# BEAUTIFULLY STOLEN

CANDIED CRUSH #4

CHARITY PARKERSON

—Warning: This book is intended for readers over the age of 18.

Copyright © 2020 Charity Parkerson
Editor: BZ Hercules & Consultants
ISBN: 978-1-946099-74-7
All rights reserved.

# INTRODUCTION

ROMAN IS TIRED OF GAMES. BRETT IS CERTAIN
THEY ARE PLAYING. ONE OF THEM IS IN FOR A
HUGE SURPRISE.

From the first moment Brett met Roman, he had the man's number. Roman is beautiful, flirtatious, and completely incapable of being loyal to anyone but himself. Everything about Roman is an act. Under normal circumstances, Brett would find a way to make money from Roman's natural ability to charm anyone. This one time, he won't, because there's just something about Roman that gets under his skin. Brett can't explain it. He simply knows Roman is trouble. Brett can't let himself fall for the game.

Roman wants Brett. That's the truth of things. Since the first time he set eyes on the eccentric ball of energy, Roman has pulled out every weapon in his arsenal to try to win him. Brett isn't into him at all. That's a first for Roman. He can't stop coming back for more of Brett's special brand of rejection. It's too sexy to resist.

When Brett invites Roman to be his date for a wedding, Roman knows the invitation is too good to be true. He just can't figure out Brett's new angle. That doesn't mean he intends to miss his chance to get shot down again. After all, he might finally win. Little does Roman know, Brett needs him way more than he could have dreamed, and they'll both be less if he can't win.

# ONE

THE CREAM-COLORED ENVELOPE CAME SPECIAL delivery. Brett stared at the expensive stationery for much longer than necessary. He knew what was inside. With nothing else for it, Brett opened the card. Even knowing what was inside didn't lessen the impact while reading the words.

*As part of their chosen family*
*Izaak 'Wrecker' Lewis*
*and*
*Johnny Wayne Savage*
*Request the honor of your presence as they tie the knot*
*Saturday the eighth day of August at two o'clock in*
*the afternoon*
*The Back Porch*

*Main Park*
*Los Angeles, California*

Brett read the invitation three times. He felt... something. Brett just wasn't sure what. On the down low, Brett had been dating Wrecker before Wrecker fell in love with Johnny. Actually, "dating" might be too strong of a word. They had been sleeping together. While they had been more than fuck buddies, they had been less than a couple. Brett didn't know if what they had been had a label exactly, but he had cared about Wrecker. Johnny was Brett's client. Brett considered him a friend. This wedding put Brett in an awkward position, to say the least.

Xavier strolled into the room. His hard, tan body almost distracted Brett from his depression. Beautiful men were his biggest weakness and he loved to watch.

Brett forced a smile to his lips. "Hello, sexy. Would you like to attend a wedding with me?"

Xavier's gray eyes had a cool edge to them, showing his true nature. "No. I can't think of anything I would like to do less than attend a wedding. With anyone. It's nothing personal."

Brett got it. He didn't like weddings either, but

2

he didn't feel like this one was one he could skip. There was one person he could call. Everything inside Brett cringed at the idea, but he knew one guy who would look ridiculously sexy next to him. One of Brett's first clients, Falcon, had gotten married almost a year ago. Falcon's husband Mason had a best friend who would do just about anything for the right price. Since Roman was otherworldly beautiful, people often threw money and gifts his way, hoping for a second of Roman's time. Brett had lots of money. He could afford to keep things impersonal while not looking pitiful at Wrecker's wedding. No doubt everyone who frequented The Back Porch would be there. Brett couldn't go while looking forlorn. Everyone there would be watching his every move, looking for any cracks to whisper about behind their hands.

Before Brett could change his mind, he quickly found Roman's number and dialed. When Roman hadn't answered by the fourth ring, Brett almost hung up. Then Roman's sexy voice caressed Brett's ear. "Hello?"

Brett had to take a steadying breath. He could already picture Roman's perfect body and long blond hair. "This is Brett. I have a proposition for you."

"*Mhmm.*" The sexy hum had Brett's eyes falling

3

closed. "Have you come around and seen the error of your ways? Have you finally decided to share my bed?"

A snort escaped Brett. He didn't want to enjoy Roman's constant flirting and ridiculousness, but Roman was irresistible. "Not that type of proposition." Xavier chuckled as he passed. Brett ignored him, as much as anyone could ignore Xavier's naked perfection. "How would you like another free trip to California? I need a date to Wrecker and Johnny's wedding."

"Interesting. Are you asking me on a date or bribing me?"

"I'm trying to hire your services." Brett was determined to keep this professional.

A sexy and evil-sounding chuckle caressed Brett's ear. "I'll hear your offer."

Brett gave a sharp nod, even though Roman couldn't see him. He felt certain they could come to terms. "Five grand and you can choose your hotel for the weekend."

"Three and I'll stay with you."

"Are you negotiating *down* with me?" Even Brett heard the confusion in his voice. He couldn't understand why Roman would ask for less money and give up his chance to stay at any of the world's most gorgeous locations.

Roman sighed. "I'd do it for free, if you asked properly, but since you didn't..."

A growl rose in Brett's throat. He refused to let it fly and give Roman the satisfaction of knowing he burrowed under Brett's skin. "This isn't a date. It's a job. Will you take it? Yes or no?"

"Six hundred dollars. I stay with you and I get to kiss you three times at any time of my choosing."

Brett's eyes fell closed. Roman was impossible. "Oh, for fuck's sake. Fine."

Roman hummed again—like satisfied. "Now, tell me everything. How would you like me to dress? When is this happening?"

Without thought, Brett laughed. The craziness of his current situation struck him. He didn't understand how he always seemed to end up in the most fucked-up situations. "I didn't realize I hadn't told you a date or anything. Yet you still accepted."

"I told you all you had to do was ask properly and I would've said yes for free. Whatever you need. It's nothing for me to rearrange my schedule for you."

Brett heard the smile in Roman's voice. He found

himself forgetting he spoke to a serial seducer. Roman was an exotic dancer by trade. Everything he did, he did to tantalize. His long blond hair and hard body. His practiced smile and seductive glances. Everything about Roman was a show. Brett always tried to stay immune. He simply wasn't sure anyone was truly insusceptible. Still, Brett didn't have to let Roman know he tempted Brett. "The wedding is Saturday, August eighth. I thought maybe I could fly you in Friday night and back home on Monday. That way, you can enjoy your trip and not spend the entire weekend traveling or attending the wedding of people you barely know."

Roman turned serious. "That's fine. I can't wait to see you. How are you holding up with this whole wedding thing?"

It was funny. Even though they hadn't been technically dating, lots of people had known Brett had been sleeping with Wrecker for a long time. Yet not one mutual friend had asked how Brett felt. The one person Brett expected to care the least—the one who didn't even know about Brett's time with Wrecker—was the one asking about his feelings. "I'm fine. They're in love and all that mess. We should all be happy, right?"

"It's a bit sickening, isn't it? The way everyone's getting married all of a sudden. I mean, I never thought Mason would take that plunge. Yet, here we are. He's married and barely speaks to me any longer. But—like I said—I can't wait to see you. That makes a wedding worthwhile. Not to mention, I bet you look sexy as hell all decked out in your finest."

Brett felt the same way about Roman. No doubt, every eye would be turned his way. The jealousy in the room would be thick. The thing was, Brett would know he paid Roman to be there. The pride he felt with Roman at his side would be tainted by that knowledge. Everyone would be looking at Brett, thinking he had landed this sexy-as-hell man, but Brett would know the truth. "I would very much like for you to go as my date. Properly, that is. If you have time for me?" Brett held his breath. He had no idea what drove him to do such a horrifying thing. This had not been his intention in any way, shape, or form when he called Roman. Roman would eat him for breakfast.

"I would be honored." If Roman had sounded smug at all, Brett might have taken back the question. Instead, Roman truly sounded every bit as honored as he claimed.

Roman's tone had Brett scrambling in other ways. "I'll still pay for your flight and you can still stay with me and all that."

"Don't worry. I can afford a plane ticket. You're worth it to me."

For a moment, Brett couldn't find his voice. He recognized that Roman was full of shit and this desire to spend time with Brett was an act. Still, Roman made it very easy to suspend reality and believe. Brett imagined Roman made a lot of money at his job. He charmed people with such ease. "Text me your flight info and I'll pick you from the airport."

"I accept your sacrifice. No one likes going to LAX."

A smile snapped to Brett's lips. Roman was a breath of fresh air. Most people didn't admit to hating it when their friends got married and picking people up from the airport. Roman said those things with no fear. "I'll look for your text."

"I'll look for your fine ass in the airport," Roman retorted.

Brett shook his head and ended their call without saying goodbye. He bit his bottom lip, trying to stop smiling. He was such an idiot. There had always been something irresistible about Roman, but seriously, Brett had really gone off the deep end this time. The phone vibrated in his hand. Brett dropped his gaze.

Roman: *I'll overlook the fact that you hung up on me and simply say it was good to hear your voice.*

With a chuckle, Brett covered his eyes. He could not let this man-child get underneath his skin. People were never nice for no reason. With Brett, people usually hoped to use him to get famous, since that was his forte. Brett could film a houseplant and find a way to market it all the way to acclaim. He didn't know why he was this way. Brett had simply always been good at putting the perfect spin on things and placing it on display in the exact spot it belonged. He could find an audience for anything. While doing what he loved brought him immense satisfaction, it also brought fake people into his life in droves. Men rarely met him accidentally and they were genuine with him even fewer times than that. He supposed that was why he had enjoyed Wrecker's company so much. Wrecker was already famous and had never wanted anything from him beyond the carnal. It was a catch twenty-two, to be honest. While Wrecker had only wanted sex and nothing more, Brett wanted to be wanted for more than what he could do for someone's career. There was no in between. No one who wanted nothing from him wanted him for him.

No doubt Roman was no different. Brett hadn't quite deciphered Roman's game yet, but he would.

Since meeting Roman nearly a year ago, the guy hadn't stopped flirting. At Johnny's first and only live event, Roman had point blank confessed he intended to fuck Brett. In truth, if Brett thought for a second that was all there was to it, he would hop in Roman's bed so fast, it would make the man's head spin, but something didn't feel right. There was something else in Roman's eyes when he looked at Brett. Almost a greediness. Brett didn't want to find out Roman's secrets the hard way. So he kept the guy at arm's length. A weekend together might finally solve the mystery of Roman, and Brett looked forward to the challenge. It wasn't like he had anything better holding his attention. He had time for this.

# TWO

CALIFORNIA HAD ITS GOOD POINTS. IN FACT, Roman had lived here once upon a time. In his early twenties, he had moved to L.A. for six months and did a stint on a soap opera. His character had only been temporary. He had known from the beginning they intended to kill off his character in the show. That six months had broken him from any more dreams of making it big. While he knew selling the sight of his body wasn't something he could do forever, at least he got to be himself when he wasn't working. In those six months of acting, Roman had been on stage twenty-four seven. No matter where he went or what he did, he had to be someone else. He had to mind his reputation every second. Roman lived with a fake smile permanently etched on his face. By the time he moved back to Aspen, he was so tired of smiling that he hadn't done it again for nearly a year. It was like the life had been sapped from him. The first time he had smiled again for real, he had sworn to himself that he would never fake it again. If he was unhappy, Roman changed his circumstances. He refused to feel that way even one more time. Maybe that was why he was so obsessed with Brett.

Everyone knew Brett Sanders in L.A. Yet, no one did. His ability to turn everything he touched to gold was envied by all. People practically spoke about him in whispers. Brett was small but fierce. He dressed like a supervillain and stood out everywhere he went. The guy had the most beautiful dark blue eyes Roman had ever seen. They were also the saddest. Brett was exactly like Roman had been in L.A.— fucking miserable. Maybe no one else saw it, or hell, maybe it was just that no one else cared. Either way, Roman saw, and he couldn't stop finding excuses to be near him. This time, though, Brett had called him. Roman could be thick sometimes, but he wasn't dumb. Only a stupid man would miss his chance at a weekend with Brett.

At the airport, Roman fully expected Brett to back down and only send a car. In fact, once he grabbed his luggage, he started searching for a sign with his name. He had zero expectations of seeing Brett's face waiting.

"You cut off all your hair."

Roman spun at the yelled words behind him. Brett stood waiting. Unlike usual, he wasn't boldly dressed. Instead of the wild makeup and even wilder colors he came to expect from Brett, Brett wore jeans and a t-shirt. His hair was still a stylish mess, but the rest of him was subdued.

Roman had never possessed an ounce of chill. Happiness roared through him at the sight of Brett. Without thought, he lifted Brett off his feet in a bear hug. "It's so good to see you. I didn't really think you'd come."

"You cut off all your hair," Brett calmly repeated like Roman didn't have him squashed against his chest and dangling a foot off the ground.

Roman set Brett back on his feet. "Yeah. I've been wanting to do it for a while. This wedding gave me the perfect excuse. Now I can look like someone who belongs at your side."

Brett's forehead furrowed. His expression screamed annoyance. "You've always looked that way. You shouldn't care what other people think. People are dumb."

He found Brett delightful. Brett was too serious

and fucking adorable. "You're incredibly sexy when you're scowling at me. Obviously, I think you're gorgeous all the time, but you're especially irresistible when you're irritated with me."

Brett's expression cleared. He shook his head. "I always forget how completely ridiculous you are."

Roman couldn't stop smiling. "It's mind-boggling. I know."

Brett released a heavy sigh. "Are you ready to get out of here? This place is fucking packed."

"Ready to rush me to bed already, are you? Let's go, then."

For a moment, Brett's eyes fell closed—like Roman made him tired. Roman's smile grew. Brett needed someone under his skin. Roman truly believed, if Brett was honest with himself, he would admit that was the real reason he had asked Roman to join him this weekend. After all, there was no way Brett didn't have a thousand men in California lined up to date him. Yet, he had called Roman. He had called the right person. Roman leaned in and kissed Brett. It was a quick brush of lips on lips. Just enough to get Brett's attention.

Brett's eyebrows shot to his hairline. "What the fuck was that?"

"My first kiss. You still owe me two more. I

promise I'll make those better. But we're in public, you know?"

The scowl was back. "You said if I asked you properly, then you would do this weekend for free."

Roman nodded. "And I am. You're not paying me. But you also said I could still stay with you and all that. My three kisses fall under the 'all that' umbrella."

Brett rolled his eyes and turned away.

Roman followed on his heels, smiling like an idiot. He couldn't wait to have Brett alone. Brett led him to a waiting Aston Martin DBS Superleggera. It was red. It was beautiful, and Roman imagined it was also fast and expensive. He tried to temper his reaction. After all, Roman's best friend had married an extremely rich man. It wasn't like he had never been exposed to ridiculous wealth. In truth, he didn't like thinking about how far out of his league Brett seemed to be. That detail was hard to ignore while climbing into the passenger side of a car worth more than he made in a year.

"If you're interested, we'll run by the house so you can drop off your stuff and do whatever, then I'll take you to dinner."

"Sounds good." Roman couldn't believe how nonchalant he sounded. In truth, he couldn't wait to be underneath Brett's roof. Being in his house meant being close to his bed, and that was where Roman fully intended to be by the end of this trip. Brett obviously had no idea how to handle Roman. Roman knew why. Brett had never met anyone as relentless as him once Roman had his mind set. Since the first time he met Brett, Roman's mind had been completely locked on owning him. This weekend was his chance. Roman wouldn't fail. Brett was already taken. He just didn't know it yet.

Now that Roman was here, Brett's nerves were frayed. He never got nervous. Brett had no clue what it was about Roman that got to him so much. As he led Roman into his assigned bedroom, Brett couldn't shake the definite flutter in his stomach. They were feet from a king-sized bed. Brett couldn't deny he wanted to jump right into it.

Brett motioned around the room as he turned to face Roman. "Here you go. The bathroom is through there." He pointed toward the open bathroom door. "If you need the wi-fi password, I'll send you a picture of the back of the router. Otherwise, there's no way I can remember that long jumble of numbers and letters. Do you need anything else?"

Roman's hazel gaze never wavered from Brett, making the timorous shake in his stomach even worse. Brett fought the urge to shift from foot to foot and rattle on like a nitwit beneath Roman's intense stare. Roman draped his garment bag across the chair by the door before parking his suitcase beside it. He crossed the room. Brett took a step back. As Roman got closer, he took another. The backs of his legs hit the bed, stopping him from getting away. A wicked glint entered Roman's eyes.

"I'm claiming my second kiss."

That was all the warning Brett got before he found himself on his back with Roman's huge body hovering over him. Roman was merciless. His kiss... expert. In fact, Brett had never experienced anything like it. Roman's tongue curled, licking and teasing. He made love to Brett with only a kiss. Brett's entire body burned. His cock strained for the same attention Roman gave his tongue. Roman licked and nipped. Sucked. Brett lost all sense of reason. Time passed with no end in sight. Brett wondered if he would come in his jeans. He had never been so thoroughly seduced. Brett questioned if he should shove Roman away before things went too far. He didn't have the strength. Brett had kissed a lot of men over the years. There was no comparison.

Brett grasped for some semblance of control. "You only asked for a kiss. No touching," Brett said between kisses. He sounded every bit as turned on as he felt. There was no hiding his desire.

"I'm not touching you."

Brett glanced down the line of his body. Roman kept his weight balanced on his hands and knees. No part of him touched Brett but his lips. That was odd. Brett would have sworn Roman's body moved against his. "Oh."

Roman reclaimed his mouth. This time, Brett did more than accept his fate. He embraced it. Maybe Roman's kiss proved what Brett had always believed. Roman had a skill only kissing a thousand men could achieve, but Brett had known that going in. When he invited Roman this weekend, Brett had known he wouldn't be special. Damned if Roman's kiss didn't trick his mind. He felt exceptional. Brett felt desired, like no one else had ever managed. He wanted Roman. Brett had always thought Roman was extremely sexy. Even after cutting off the long hair Brett loved so damn much, Brett still thought Roman was the most gorgeous man he had ever set eyes on. With that said, he had never had any intention of touching the man in any way. Now, he couldn't stop. All Roman had to do was make a move and Brett would cave. He was at peace with that decision.

Roman's kiss turned sweet. He lightly swept his lips across Brett's, making Brett's heart squeeze. "So sweet," Roman whispered, making it a little harder for Brett to breathe. "You make me want to stay right here forever. Thank you for not pushing me away." Roman brushed noses with Brett before pushing to his feet. There was no missing the bulge in Roman's jeans, but he obviously didn't intend to act on things. "Just let me cool down and we'll go."

Brett couldn't find his voice to respond. He blinked at the ceiling, trying to breathe through the lust. The unquenched desire wasn't the worst part, even though that was awful. As always, the truth was Brett's worst enemy. He liked Roman. Brett hadn't wanted that. Nothing good could come of longing for Roman. Not his time and not his touch. Even if Roman didn't live nine hundred miles away, Roman wasn't the type to settle down. Brett didn't have the time or mental spoons for anyone anyhow. He didn't want to take away from his work—the one thing that kept him sane—to invest in someone else who would never love him. People never loved Brett. He was the guy people passed the time with while they waited to find the one. Brett was never the one. That was a kick to the teeth. Brett didn't want to feel that way with Roman. Roman had too many irresistible qualities. He was fun and funny. Roman always smiled and joked. Flirted. He tempted and teased people into happiness. Roman wasn't meant for someone like Brett. Brett was too serious and driven. Roman deserved to have someone who made him smile.

Roman laughed, pulling Brett's focus his way. A bright smile lit Roman's flushed face. "You look like you're mentally grading me. Was it that bad?"

"I just remembered I forgot to email a client."

A roar of laughter rent the air. Roman's light didn't dim one iota at Brett's claim. "Come on." He pulled Brett to his feet. "Let's go get dinner before I waste my final kiss only to remind you of more work you're forgetting."

Brett's gaze dropped to Roman's mouth at the threat of another kiss. He truly hadn't invited Roman here for this. "Your kiss gets an A minus."

Roman's laughter was addictive. Brett didn't want it to stop. "And I'm jet-lagged. Imagine what I can do at full bars."

Fuck. Brett couldn't even imagine. He didn't stand a chance. The bed was too close. They had to get out of there. Brett had never been in so much danger in his life. He absolutely couldn't wait to see what happened next.

———

ROMAN HADN'T INTENDED TO WASTE HIS SECOND kiss so quickly. He hadn't exactly squandered it. His body was on fire and he almost hurt, he wanted Brett so badly. But he hadn't planned to use all three kisses in one night. Roman had thought to spread them out throughout the weekend, getting the most out of them for his planned seduction. Unfortunately, seeing Brett's house had left him feeling insecure. He had to showcase some serious skill if he had any hopes of enticing someone like Brett.

Brett didn't have a house. He had a fucking estate. Hidden behind a stone fence, Brett's home had a humongous garage, a gigantic swimming pool complete with water falls and landscaping to make it look like a jungle watering hole. As they had cleared the back door and cut through a mud room, Roman had caught sight of his dream kitchen. Roman loved to cook, eat, and cook what he loved to eat. Brett's kitchen was a chef's wet dream. There were multiple ovens and cooktops. Cabinets as far as the eye could see. His refrigerator looked big enough to walk inside. Roman had to force himself not to go exploring like a little kid. Instead, he had kept his gaze locked on Brett, refusing temptation. Unfortunately, staring at Brett wasn't a better option. The guy was just so fucking delicious, and that kiss... damn. Roman was so blown away that happiness had him laughing at every little thing. Brett was amazing. Roman needed more.

Roman didn't manage to hide his love for Brett's kitchen the second time they passed through. "How do you feel about me cooking for you sometime this weekend?"

Brett glanced over his shoulder. "You're my guest."

Roman couldn't fight his excitement. "Then you should definitely let me have my way. This kitchen is amazing. I love to cook, and I'm pretty damn good at it, if I do say so myself. That Dacor is calling my name. You have to let me showcase my skills."

Brett led Roman back to his car. "I don't know what that is."

"It's a range. You have it in your kitchen. Didn't you pick it out?" He really didn't understand rich people sometimes. Money was wasted on the wealthy.

Brett shrugged as he opened his car door. "My neighbor helped design my kitchen when I remodeled a few months ago. He's a chef, so I just trusted him to make it the best. Now I'm glad I did. Your excitement is adorable. Feel free to go wild while you're here. Cook until your heart is content."

Roman had to stop himself from rubbing his hands together maniacally. He would start with breakfast. Maybe even breakfast in bed. Brett might have a huge house and tons of money, but Roman had his own seduction arsenal. Roman found himself sinking into his thoughts while Brett drove. He wondered if it would be rude to raid Brett's fridge and take stock, in case he needed to get some items delivered before morning. Brett stopped at a red light. Roman glanced over. Brett's arm rested on the arm rest. That smoking hot kiss flared to life in Roman's mind again, refusing to be held at bay any longer by the thoughts of food. Brett would be amazing in Roman's bed. He couldn't wait to have this sexy man straddling his hips.

Roman ran his fingertips down Brett's arm, savoring the sensation of Brett's soft skin without thought. When he reached Brett's hand, Roman brought it to his mouth and kissed the back. With his eyes closed, he inhaled Brett's scent. He smelled familiar. Nostalgia washed over him, but he couldn't place the scent. Brett leaned his way and kissed Roman's cheek. Roman turned his head, capturing Brett's lips. Their lips clung, sweetly lingering. Roman craved. There was no other word for it. Brett made him want things he had never cared about before. Roman couldn't explain it.

"You're not seducing me," Brett said, pulling away. Brett stared at him so long that Roman almost forgot where they were. He swallowed the desire choking him. "I know." He really did. Brett was the one seducing him. "The light is green."

Brett looked away and went. The world exploded. The air left Roman's lungs as something slammed into his face. He fought to breathe as pain vibrated through him and screeching metal assailed his ears. He fought his way through the white cloud attacking him and sucked air. There was a horn that wouldn't stop blowing. When the haze finally cleared, Roman's confusion evaporated. They had been hit. Fear slammed into him as he caught sight of Brett. He was slumped over the steering wheel, unmoving. Roman quickly unsnapped his seatbelt and reached for Brett. He moved slow, hoping not to make any injuries worse. Brett was limp—like there was no life in his body. Blood covered his face and poured from his nose. Roman checked his pulse. It felt strong. He didn't hesitate to peel off his shirt and use it to stem the blood running freely down Brett's face.

"It's okay, baby. I've got you. Wake up. We need to get out of this car."

People swarmed the car, trying to open Roman's door. Someone knocked on the window and asked if they were okay. Everything was a low hum on the outskirts of his panic. Brett wasn't regaining consciousness and the entire driver's side was caved in. A large dark-colored truck was parked where the steering wheel should have been. The more Roman's mind cleared, the worse things looked. He threw open his door and scrambled onto his knees, trying to unbuckle Brett's seat belt. It took some doing, but he managed to cram his hand in between Brett's body and the center console to get it undone. Things were way closer to Brett than they should have been. With so much damage, he worried the car might catch fire and there was no way Brett could get out through his side.

Brett suddenly screamed out in pain—like he went from unconscious to waking up in hell in an instant.

Roman pressed his lips to Brett's forehead, trying

to cling to sanity. "I'm here. I've got you. Tell me what hurts."

In a panic, Brett tried looking around. He fought Roman while coming to grips with reality. "Goddamn. I'm stuck. I can't move my legs." The more Brett struggled and the more his terror grew, the more helpless Roman became. Sirens filled the air and Roman prayed for them to get closer while trying his best to keep Brett calm.

"Shhh. Help is coming."

Brett's dark blue gaze latched on to Roman. He held Roman's stare and visibly fought for sanity. Roman clung to him, trying to keep him calm. Brett tried to move again. Another cry escaped him, ratcheting up Roman's fear. Brett went limp—like the life left his body again. Roman fought the urge to scream for help. He didn't know what to do. Roman had never been more terrified in his life. Time creeped by, making him feel like help would never arrive while Brett suffered from god only knew what injuries. He needed Brett to be okay. They still had things to discuss. Memories to make. Brett had countless people who looked to him for a bright future. Roman would keep him safe. He would make him better. If it was the last thing he did, Roman would see Brett smile again.

## THREE

THE INSIDE OF BRETT'S MOUTH FELT LIKE HE had been licking shag carpeting for hours. His eyes were gritty as he peeled them open. He hadn't felt this bad since the last time he got the flu. The more he rejoined the world of the living, the less he wanted to be there. Everything hurt. Not just a little —like he had slept wrong, but a lot—like he had been hit by a fast-moving truck. Oh yeah. He had. The hazy memory of Roman keeping him calm creeped into Brett's brain. His foot had been pinned and felt like a shark had mistaken it for a meal. Brett tried wiggling his toes. A gasp escaped him as a searing pain ran up his leg.

The moment the sound left his lips, Roman was

there, hovering over him. "Are you okay? Do I need to call the nurse?"

Brett blinked, trying to make Roman's words make sense. He looked harder at his surroundings. There was an IV nearby. Fuck. He was in the hospital. "Is my foot still attached?"

At his croaked question, a smile exploded across Roman's face. "Yeah. It's still there, but you might wish it wasn't for a couple of months. It's got some new hardware. Pins and screws. Good luck getting through airport security from now on. Your nurse said if you wake up hurting to let her know. She can bring you the good stuff."

Brett glanced around, still trying to get his bearings. "Can you lift this bed or something? I'm feeling disoriented."

Roman quickly moved to help. He pushed the button, easing the head of the bed upward.

"That's good," Brett gasped when all his injuries made themselves known. He could feel his pulse pounding in several places. His face and entire left side felt like a baseball bat had enjoyed its game, using him as the ball. He tried focusing on Roman instead of his pain. Roman wore scrubs. That caught Brett's attention. "Why are you in scrubs?"

"You bled all over my clothes," Roman answered,

sounding absent as he grabbed a cup of ice water and offered Brett a drink. While Brett gratefully sipped, Roman kept talking. "Your car is obviously totaled, and you've been out of it for close to thirty-six hours. All my things are at your place, so a guy on the night shift let me borrow some clothes."

Guilt washed over Brett. "Jesus. I'm so sorry. Wait. Thirty-six hours? We missed the wedding and I ruined your trip."

Roman rolled his eyes. "You did not ruin my trip. Some asshole running from the cops ruined our weekend." A sexy smirk touched his lips. "I hate that you're hurt, but I kind of like having you at my mercy."

It was Brett's turn to roll his eyes. Now that he was somewhat lucid, he tried taking stock. He eyed his body. There was a thick bandage covering his left foot and ankle, stopping him from seeing the damage. Considering the rest of his left leg was completely black, he didn't think he needed to see. The way his face hurt left him with a bad feeling it looked the same as his leg. This put a definite damper on his upcoming schedule. A million and one things he had planned raced through his mind at once. Thirty-six hours in the hospital meant he was a day and a half behind on work. Defeat washed over him.

"Don't look like that. I'm here. Put me to work. I'll help you do whatever needs to be done."

Brett's gaze swung back Roman's way. He swore sometimes the man could read his mind. A small bruise on the outside corner of Roman's eye caught Brett's attention. His heart raced with a sudden burst of fear. He found himself inspecting Roman, looking for more injuries. "How are you, by the way? Did you get hurt? Are you okay?"

"I'm good." Roman sounded calm and steady. "Seeing you get hurt took ten years off my life that I couldn't spare, but I'm fine."

Brett's heart rate slowed. As his panic ebbed, the guilt skyrocketed. "Let me hire a car to take you back to my place. In fact, I'll cover a first-class ticket so you can head home and I'll pay you the fee we originally discussed. Obviously, I never meant for this to happen, and I'm incredibly sorry."

The longer Brett spoke, the harder Roman's expression got, until Brett trailed off. The moment he went silent, Roman stepped in. "If you're through, this is what we're doing. You'll make me a list of what you need from the house and what work you need done. I'll go take care of everything on the list. Your doctor will tell you when you can go home and your limitations. Then I'll go home with you and make sure you stick to his orders. So you can stop apologizing because that's just ridiculous."

Brett was in pain. His head spun and he didn't feel good in any sense of the word. The strength it would take to argue wasn't there and probably wouldn't be for a while. The least he could do was make sure Roman was cared for. "Did my phone survive?"

With a snort and a shake of his head, Roman crossed the room, grabbed Brett's phone, and passed it his way. Brett didn't have much battery left and his screen was cracked, but he accomplished his task.

While staring at the phone and clicking around, Brett gave in as gracefully as he could. "If you're determined to do this, I could really use some pain meds, because I'm pretty sure I'm dying. Also, I'm sending you a list via text of things I need." He clicked send and focused on Roman. "I just ordered an Uber for you. When you get to the house, type three seven six on the keypad and that will unlock the door. In the cabinet closest to the doorway in the kitchen, there are keys to my cars. Pick one to use while you're here. There's a black card in my wallet. Get it. You can use that to buy whatever you need." If Roman had looked triumphant, Brett might have stopped and saved his pride. Instead, Roman stood there looking ready to jump in and Brett felt... something. "Thank you for everything."

Roman nodded. "We're friends. You would do the same for me."

Brett didn't know if that was true. Honestly, he wasn't sure anymore what friendship felt like. It had been a long time since anyone had anything to do with him where they weren't also wanting something from him. Maybe that was a street that went both ways. Brett also didn't bother with anyone he wasn't working with to further their careers. It was possible he didn't know how to be anyone's friend. Roman didn't look at him like a friend. In fact, he watched Brett in a way that didn't feel friendly in the least. He didn't know what he felt with Roman around. For whatever reason, though, he didn't want it to stop. So he would let Roman help. Maybe he would regret it. Maybe he wouldn't. Only time would tell. At the end of the day, if Roman turned out to be like everyone else, it wouldn't be the first time anyone had used him, and likely wouldn't be the last. At least Roman was here now. That was more than he could say about anyone else.

---

Brett owned a black Range Rover that looked like it needed driving. Between Brett's list and a much-needed shower, things were taking longer than Roman liked. Every time he thought about Brett's seemingly lifeless body in his arms while first responders worked to free him from the car, Roman's stomach started shaking all over again. He needed to get back to Brett. Roman had to admit that snooping through Brett's room—looking for everything on his list—had been fun… and informative.

Brett didn't own any nude magazines or visible porn. His room was a clean mess. Like there weren't any dirty clothes or any trash strewn about, but nothing was folded in his drawers, his bed was unmade, and his closet was a disaster area. The rest of the house was meticulous, giving Roman the impression Brett had a housekeeper, but it seemed he didn't allow them inside his bedroom. Roman wondered if anyone besides Brett was ever inside Brett's room. Judging by Brett's bedside table, he had the means to please himself. Roman kept smiling at the stash of toys Brett kept. That was definitely one detail Roman could use to add to his already vivid fantasies of Brett.

With a bag packed, Roman headed back to the

hospital. He had forgotten how much he hated L.A. traffic, but damn, Brett's Range Rover was nice. It beat the hell out of his twenty-year-old Camry. Roman couldn't afford to get new car fever. His house and car were paid for and he couldn't take his clothes off for money forever. In fact, he had really passed the age most people stopped like five years ago. The thing was he wasn't good at anything and life hadn't exactly been what he hoped. At nineteen, he had thought he would be famous. When that didn't turn out the way he hoped, Roman had decided to lean heavily upon the only thing he had going for him. His looks. Roman wasn't conceited. At least, he didn't think he was. He was old enough to know that looks faded and being considered handsome wasn't a talent. Roman knew men in their sixties who still made a lot of money from being silver foxes. At thirty-nine, Roman already knew he wouldn't be one of those guys. He was already tired by ten every night and hated working until two each morning. The most depressing part of it all was that he thought he would have found himself by now. Everyone else his age seemed to have their shit together. Not Roman. He just didn't have any real talents. Coming back to L.A. always reminded him of that.

By the time Roman weaved his way through the hospital parking lot, heading for the door, the depression he always barely kept at bay threatened to pour in. He never knew when it would strike. That was why he loved making other people smile so much. When he made other people happy, that was the only time Roman felt good about himself.

A loud whistle rent the air. "Yo. Roman."

Roman's steps faltered at the sound of his name being called. He looked over his shoulder to find a group of four men headed his way. He recognized three of the men, even though he had only met two. Roman had met Johnny and Wrecker the last time he came to L.A. to see Johnny's concert. Well, truthfully, he had come to see Brett, and Johnny was Brett's client, so the concert had been the perfect excuse. Of the three men headed his way, the only human-sized man squeezed between all the huge bodies was the one Roman couldn't tear his gaze from. It was Jessie Thunder. Roman couldn't even blink. He had met a lot of semi-famous people over the years, but Jessie was a legend. A rock-and-roll god. Everyone knew his name and face and he was headed Roman's way.

The moment they reached his side, Johnny jumped in, talking a mile a minute. "I almost didn't recognize you with your short hair. How is Brett? We heard about his accident on the news and I tried calling, but he didn't answer. I don't know what room he's in or anything, but the news said he's here. I'm glad to see you. Jessie came with us in case we had to leverage star power to find out his room number, but running into you makes things so much easier."

Roman had to force his gaze away from Jessie. "Um, yeah. He's okay. I'm headed up now if you want to come with me." They all headed inside together while Roman kept filling in the blanks. "He was pinned in the crash, so he ended up with a crushed foot and ankle. They put it all back together, but he'll be down for a while." Johnny hissed but didn't interrupt. "His nose is broken, and his entire left side is black with bruises. Before I left to get him some things from the house, they pumped him full of pain meds, so he's probably sleeping. I imagine that's why he didn't answer when you called." Roman met Johnny's stare. "He was really upset about missing your wedding. I had to make him stop apologizing. Congratulations, by the way." As Wrecker and Johnny thanked him, Roman lost his ability to pretend any longer. He focused on Jessie. "I'm Roman. I'm a huge fan."

A sweet-looking smile touched Jessie's lips. Roman lost his breath. Jessie looked... kind. Roman never could have anticipated that. "It's nice to meet you. I'm glad Brett has someone taking care of him. To be honest, I half expected to get here and find out he had checked himself out of the hospital. He doesn't strike me as the type to tolerate any interruption to his schedule. No matter what."

A laugh burst from Roman. "If I wasn't here, you'd be right. He was half out of it this morning and he still managed to write me a list of work he needs done today while hiring a car to drive me home. I don't know how he could see his phone with all the drugs pumping through him, but he has shit to do. He wasn't letting this hold him down."

Johnny released a loud sigh. "Yep. That sounds like him."

Roman glanced between Wrecker and Johnny as they stepped off the elevator and onto Brett's floor. "Aren't you two going on a honeymoon or something?"

Wrecker nodded and answered for them. "We're headed to Maine in the morning. I own a business and it's not as easy to walk away from as I'd like."

"What type of business?" Honestly, Roman was merely making conversation.

"The Back Porch. It's a coffeehouse," Johnny answered for Wrecker, sounding proud.

"*The* coffeehouse of L.A.," the fourth man said, speaking up for the first time. "Everyone goes there."

Roman focused on the guy. He was so damn big that Roman had thought he was probably only a guard. Roman realized he was being rude. "I'm sorry. I'm Roman," Roman said, introducing himself again. "My mind is kind of all over the place right now. Sorry I didn't introduce myself sooner. Between getting hit by a truck, watching Brett suffer while they cut him from the car, and not really sleeping since, I'm barely functioning at this point."

The huge dude nodded. "It's cool. I'm Declan. My husband is one of Brett's clients. He wanted to be here, but he ended up sick after the wedding and he didn't want to bring any germs to Brett's room. He made me come so I can tell him every detail. Plus, I have to keep Jessie safe."

There was a lot to unpack there and Roman had questions, but they were standing outside Brett's room. Roman realized he should probably warn Brett he was about to be besieged. "Just let me pop in and make sure he's decent or whatever."

Everyone nodded and it hit Roman. No one questioned his right to be the one in charge of Brett's care. Even though each of them probably had more right to watch over Brett than he did, they accepted Roman as the most important person in Brett's life. That was every bit as sad as it was moving. It was as if Brett had no one who considered themselves close enough to take care of him. That was okay. Roman wanted the job.

He opened the door and peeked in before stepping all the way inside. He smiled at the first sight of Brett. It looked as if the nurse had taken good care of him while Roman had been gone. His bed had been lowered again and blankets piled on top of him. His head turned Roman's way as Roman slipped inside the room.

"Hey. That was a quick trip." Brett's voice still sounded rough.

Roman set his overnight bag aside. "I was in a hurry to get back to your gorgeous face." Brett snorted. Roman didn't let that slow him. "You have some visitors waiting in the hall. Is it okay if they come in?"

Brett eyed his mound of covers, as if checking to make sure his body was still intact. "Yeah. That's fine."

Roman glanced behind him. "You're cool to come in." He grabbed the bag he had brought and moved deeper into the room, making room for everyone. Roman made his way to the corner of the room and unpacked Brett's laptop while they visited. He checked Brett's list and found the password Brett had given him to unlock the device. In a matter of minutes, he was logged in to Brett's computer. He worked his way down the list of rescheduling Brett needed. Roman emailed each client, introducing himself and explaining why Brett couldn't do any upcoming shows. With that out of the way, he checked Brett's social media accounts. Roman tuned out everything as he responded to well-wishers and updated his fans on his condition. He didn't hesitate blocking accounts that said spiteful things. Roman lost track of time as he did what he did best. He charmed people, skating the thin line of keeping Brett's personal business quiet while keeping people entertained.

"It was nice meeting you, Roman," Jessie said, interrupting him and making him realize how long he had been lost in working.

"You too." Roman nodded along as everyone said their goodbyes and wished Brett well. The moment they were alone, Roman set the computer aside and moved to check on Brett. He was barely awake.

Roman readjusted his covers and pillows before refilling his water. He turned down the lights.

"Do you need anything?" Brett asked, sounding half asleep.

Roman kissed his cheek. "Yeah. I need you to rest. I have everything else under control."

"Okay."

At Brett's barely whispered response, Roman moved back to the computer. He couldn't believe, as injured as Brett was, he still asked about Roman's comfort. While Roman might not have much to offer, he would make sure Brett was cared for in every way. He deserved that. Brett needed someone to keep his brand going while he recovered. That was something Roman could do. Roman wouldn't fail him.

## FOUR

Brett made a valiant effort to take back his independence once released from the hospital. Unfortunately, the pain, the meds, having one working leg, and Roman made that impossible. The moment he pulled into Brett's garage, Brett knew he was fucked. Roman refused to let him attempt to hobble into the house. Instead, he had easily carried Brett to bed. The moment he was settled, a wave of exhaustion washed over Brett like he hadn't been sleeping nonstop. He didn't feel rested. Nurses and everyone else under the sun had been waking him up every five minutes since he had awoken two days ago. His bed felt amazing.

"I need a shower."

"You can have a bath," Roman fussed, sounding like he was the boss.

Brett definitely felt at his mercy. "Don't you have a job to get back to or like bills to pay?"

Roman chuckled. "Falcon very generously paid off my house when he married Mason, since he stole my roommate. My car is twenty years old and is hanging on by a thread, but it's paid for too. My savings account looks fine. I'm not needed anywhere else. As much as I know it pains you to admit it, you need me here. I don't expect you to say as much, though. So, what would you like to eat? Eat first, then I'll help you into the tub."

A small growl slipped from Brett before he could stop it from happening. "I can do some things by myself."

Roman cocked his head to one side. "Can you? Like what?"

Brett thought it over as he took stock of his body. "Bring me my laptop. I can work."

A bright smile lit Roman's face—like he found Brett's words funny. "No."

A small part of Brett wanted to rage at Roman's high-handedness. The problem was that Roman looked damn sexy hovering over his bed and he had been too fucking sweet, doing everything for Brett.

Brett wouldn't make the man's life harder. In fact, he needed to find a way to make this up to Roman.

"If you bring me my phone, I'll order something to eat. You've been doing too much for me as it is."

Roman's smile didn't falter. "Nope. I love cooking and I'm pretty damn good at it. You said I could use your kitchen, so... any food allergies?"

Brett bit back an aggravated sigh. "Nope. Have fun." Brett shifted positions, trying to find a comfortable spot. A gasp escaped him.

Roman was trying to make him better before the sound died away. "Tell me how to help. More pillows? Less pillows?"

"Everything hurts." Brett hated admitting to any weaknesses. Between the wreck and sleeping in the hospital's hard bed, every bruise he had felt ten times worse today. "I really want to soak in a hot bath... and pray for death, honestly."

"Okay. Give me a minute."

Brett watched Roman head inside the bathroom with his heart in his throat. He didn't know what he would have done if Roman hadn't been with him. The guy had been a miracle. No one else would have dropped everything to revolve around Brett's needs. That fucked with Brett's head more than he wanted to admit. Roman reappeared before Brett cried. The pain meds made him weak.

"I don't want to leave you alone and you get hurt, but I will turn my back while you undress and get in the tub. That way, you can call out if you need me." Roman picked Brett up as he made the claim. The threat of tears was back at Roman's offer. He didn't understand why Roman had to be so nice. Roman confused him. Since the day they met, Brett had been certain he had Roman's number. Now it seemed he played some game Brett hadn't figured out. It left Brett off balance. No one was this nice for no reason.

Roman set him on the edge of the tub. "Is there anything you don't think you can do by yourself?"

Brett thought it over. He had dressed himself, so he didn't think he would have a problem undressing himself. The workout shorts and t-shirt he wore were baggy enough to be easy to remove around his bandages and splints. He could likely swing his right leg into the tub and ease himself in while keeping his left leg draped over the edge of the tub. Getting out would be harder, but he would cross that bridge when he came to it. "No. I guess, once I'm in, if you could find me some clean clothes, that would be great, but I think I can get in the tub alone."

With a nod, Roman turned his back and crossed his arms over his chest. Brett smiled again at the sight. The rigid way he stood screamed that he had no intention of peeking. If he had asked, Brett would have let him know he didn't care. While Brett might not strip for a living the way Roman did, he was no prude. Nor was he ashamed of his body. It was too skinny and not at all as sexy as Roman's, but his body wasn't the worst. Brett managed a lot by standing on one leg and bracing his weight with his hands until he sank into the hot water Roman had readied for him. A relieved sigh fell from his lips as the heat enveloped him. Roman glanced over his shoulder. "I'll find you something to wear."

Brett wanted to make Roman sit still, but he needed the help, and he didn't know how to convince Roman to do anything. He felt ridiculously uncomfortable. No one ever took care of him. He fought the urge to swing wildly between thanking Roman and apologizing. Brett agonized over it until Roman returned. Then Brett's mind latched on to how gorgeous Roman looked and refused to budge. He didn't want to believe Roman was as beautiful on the inside as he was the outside. That meant Brett had been wrong about Roman all along. Brett wasn't the type to misjudge. He had always been great at weighing character.

"Okay. I swear, everything you own is boujee as hell. You have next to no normal-people clothes. However, I managed to find this huge V-neck t-shirt in the back of your closet. Since you're going back to bed, I say you should just wear this and be comfortable."

Brett eyed the shirt and tried not to be offended by the "normal people" comment. He knew he wasn't like everyone else in the world. Brett didn't need that pointed out. "That's Wrecker's shirt."

Roman's steps faltered. He glanced down at the shirt and back Brett's way. "Why would you..." Brett saw the moment the pieces clicked together in Roman's mind.

An overwhelming need to explain washed over Brett. "It was before Johnny came along. Johnny doesn't know. I'd like to keep it that way."

The closed expression Roman wore gave nothing away. He turned away, tossed the shirt in the trash, and walked out. Brett blinked at the spot where Roman had been. He didn't think Roman had any reason to be jealous. Damned if that wasn't the vibe that he had gotten from Roman's reaction, though. Brett bathed and tried not to overthink things. Being clean was nice. At least Roman had left him a towel, since it seemed he had been abandoned. Brett braced his one good foot against the tub and used his upper body strength to push himself from the water. It wasn't a graceful exit. In fact, he almost fell. Somehow, he managed to end up sitting on the edge of the tub with his feet on the floor. He wrapped the towel around himself while struggling to catch his breath. Everything felt like a chore. Exhaustion sat heavy on his shoulders. He swayed.

Roman was there. "Whoa. Why didn't you call for me?"

"I'm fine." Even Brett heard the weakness in his voice. "I just need a minute."

Roman snorted. "You're so stubborn." He grabbed another towel and went to work drying Brett. Before Brett could argue, Roman stole the wet towel draped around him and tossed it aside. He looked completely detached as he helped Brett into a pair of underwear and then lifted him into his arms. Roman fascinated Brett. While he knew there was nothing sexy about being someone's caretaker, the flirt he had come to know had vanished.

Brett needed to know more. "You're missing some golden opportunities here to be vulgar."

Roman's mouth lifted in one corner in a sexy

smirk as he set Brett on the bed. "There's nothing sexy about exploiting an injured man." He tucked Brett into bed before using the covers to pin Brett to the mattress. Roman's mouth hovered an inch from Brett's lips. If he lifted his head, their lips would touch. Brett's cock twitched. Roman's breath fanned Brett's face as he spoke. "You'll come to me when you're feeling up to it." Roman pushed away, leaving Brett turned on and breathless. The pure cockiness in Roman's claim had Brett wishing he could scramble after the man. Brett had never dealt with anyone like him. And fuck if Roman wasn't right. The moment Brett had an ounce of strength, he fully intended to rock Roman's world. When Roman left here, he would always think of Brett with a smile. Brett would make sure of it.

---

THE MOMENT ROMAN STEPPED OUT OF SIGHT, HE bent at the waist and sucked air. Goddamn. Brett got under his skin. Roman fought the urge to turn around. He could protect those injuries and still fuck Brett senseless. While Brett might dress eccentric and hold his shoulders like a man who knew his worth, Roman didn't think Brett truly understood his power. Since they met, Roman hadn't pictured himself with anyone else. Helping Brett dress while he craved doing the opposite had nearly snapped his brain. It didn't help he was still slightly angry over the idea of Brett with Wrecker. Logically, Roman understood the ridiculousness of his reaction. He was no saint. Something about knowing anyone else touched Brett made his inner caveman roar. Roman shook off his mood. He needed to prove his worth.

First, he headed to Brett's office and fired the computer to life. He needed to keep Brett's social media accounts thriving. Roman gave himself thirty minutes of posting before heading toward the kitchen. Brett still needed to eat. He rummaged through the fridge, trying to force himself to keep it simple. There was a surprising amount of food in Brett's house. Almost like a gourmet chef lived there. Roman could do anything. The possibilities were endless.

"Are you robbing the place, then?"

Roman froze at the sound of the slightly accented words. He peeked around the edge of the refrigerator door. A flawlessly beautiful man with chiseled abs and zero clothes stood inside the kitchen, waiting for Roman to find his tongue. Roman knew his face. Hell, everyone knew him, but

Roman had never seen the man like this. Roman swallowed, searching for his voice.

"Um. No. I'm a friend of Brett's. I'm taking care of him."

The guy's icy gray stare moved down Roman's body before coming back to rest on his face. "Ah. You must be Roman. It's good of you to stay. Brett isn't one to ask for help. No matter how much he needs it." With that pronouncement out of the way, the dude seemed done with Roman. He stepped around Roman, as if dismissing him, and leaned inside the fridge for a drink while still acting as if he wasn't completely nude in Brett's kitchen. With a shake of his head, Roman walked away and headed back to Brett's bedroom. The moment he cleared the door, he lost his ability to stay calm.

"There's a naked dude in your kitchen."

Brett had a pillow covering his face. He lifted the corner to peek out at Roman. He looked half asleep and delicious. "That would be Xavier."

Roman blinked. "I know his name is Xavier. Everyone on the planet knows his name is Xavier, but that doesn't explain why he's in your kitchen... naked. Is this a common occurrence?"

Brett dropped the pillow, covering his face once more. His voice came out muffled from underneath.

"He's my neighbor. His house is being renovated, so he's staying with me temporarily. And yes, he's usually naked. Feel free to ignore him or tell him to put on pants. It'll be good for his ego." Brett shifted positions and a gasp escaped him. "Fuck."

Roman shot to Brett's side and tried making him better. "What's wrong? How can I help?" Roman needed Brett to get better. He hated seeing him in pain.

Brett tossed the pillow covering his face aside. "I'm tired of being on my back, but there's no way to turn on my side that doesn't hurt everything. I'm so sick of this."

Roman tried not to smile. Brett was a terrible patient and so fucking adorable. "Okay. I've got this." Roman crawled onto the bed and rearranged the pillows. He knew Brett couldn't sleep on his bruised side, but neither could he leave his injured ankle unsupported. First, he stacked the pillows where Brett could roll onto his uninjured side and keep his hurt foot elevated. Then he settled on his side, spooning Brett so he couldn't move.

A loud and relieved-sounding sigh caressed Roman's ears. "Dear god. That's good. Thank you."

Roman had to take a slow breath through his nose at Brett's tone. He imagined Brett sounded exactly the same while getting fucked. Roman tried shifting positions so his growing erection didn't poke Brett. He had no intention of molesting the man. Honestly, he only wanted to bring Brett peace. Each day he could help Brett relax, Brett got a day closer to being strong enough for independence. Roman needed Brett back on his feet so he could sweep Brett off them again. Roman couldn't stop his lips from skimming Brett's temple, cheek, and neck. He tried to keep the gestures loving rather than sexual. He was too turned on to know if he succeeded.

"Why are you being so nice to me?"

Roman froze with his lips pressed to Brett's shoulder. He didn't have a solid answer. To be honest, he didn't understand this draw he felt in Brett's company. "You're my friend," he said, deciding to go with the one thing he understood about them.

Brett's hand unexpectedly snaked between their bodies. He massaged Roman's cock through his jeans. "Are we friends?"

Roman drew an unsteady breath, unsure of how to respond.

"I'm sorry, Brett. This fellow has been banging on the door for twenty minutes."

Roman's head shot up. With all the blood

currently south of his brain, he was slow to understand they weren't alone. Two men stood in the bedroom doorway. Xavier was still nude. The other guy didn't seem to notice. He held a motorcycle helmet underneath his arm—like he always had one with him. Everything from the man's short cropped dark hair, wide shoulders, and wrinkle-free t-shirt screamed discipline. His cold blue gaze swept across the room as if taking in everything. Roman found himself sitting up, in case he needed to protect Brett.

"I guess I need to sit up too." Brett sounded adorably disgruntled. Roman went to work. He stacked pillows behind Brett so he could see his visitor. "Hey, Dean," Brett said the moment Roman had him settled against the headboard. Brett motioned Roman's way. "Roman." He motioned Xavier's way. "Xavier. This is my brother, Dean. Dean, meet Xavier and Roman."

Dean barely spared them a glance as he stepped farther into the room. Xavier followed him like tethered to the man. Dean's eyes flashed with anger. "You didn't call. I had to hear about your accident on the goddamn news."

"Same," Xavier said, as if he had the same right to be angry as Brett's brother.

Brett blew out a sigh. "I was a little busy having surgery, sleeping, and getting pumped full of drugs. I'd planned to call you later today. I'm surprised you didn't storm the hospital."

That last statement didn't look like it made things better. A muscle in Dean's jaw flexed like he ground his back teeth. "They wouldn't give me any info, so I had no clue which room you were in."

Xavier cut in again. "Same."

Brett cast an exasperated look Xavier's way. "For fuck's sake, Xavier. Put on some pants. We have guests."

"I'm a guest too," Xavier muttered under his breath.

Brett squeezed the spot between his eyes. "You would think that would be an argument for rather than against wearing pants, but here we are."

Xavier's face lit, as if an idea struck. "What are your thoughts, boys? You're the guests he's referring to. Do I have to get dressed?"

Roman shrugged. "I'm a stripper. My whole existence is being around naked men."

Xavier looked triumphant as his gaze swung Dean's way. "What about you?"

Dean barely spared Xavier a glance. "You're just another dude. Why should I care?"

For a moment, Xavier stared at Dean expressionlessly. "I'll go find pants." He walked away, giving no clue to his sudden change of heart.

The second he was gone, Brett snorted so hard that Roman's throat hurt by proxy. "You called Xavier Nilsson just another dude." Brett took an audible breath and snorted again. It took Roman a second to realize Brett was laughing so hard, the only sound he could make was snorts.

Roman smiled. His cheeks hurt. He had never seen Brett genuinely laugh. He saw it now. It was hilarious. Brett couldn't seem to catch his breath.

Dean shrugged. "So what? He is."

"Google his name." Another snort. "Google his name."

Roman didn't care who Xavier was. He couldn't take his eyes off Brett. "You're a snorter. I never would've guessed."

Brett swiped at his eyes as he visibly fought to get his laughter under control. He lost it again the moment Dean started reading Xavier's bio aloud.

"Xavier Nilsson is a Swedish-born model turned actor. Dubbed Sweden's most beautiful man, Xavier now lives in Los Angeles, California where he hosts a popular cooking show, *Cuisinier Unveiled*. He has also won several awards, including an Oscar for his role in the movie *Moved...* Wait. I've seen that one." Dean looked thoughtful for a minute, as if he searched his memory. "Oh, shit. Is Xavier the guy who goes on the killing spree?"

Brett nodded. "That's the one." Brett wiped his eyes again and sighed. "This was fun. You don't come by often enough."

Dean scowled. In that moment, Roman saw the resemblance between the brothers. "You're never home."

Brett didn't back down. "You have my number. All you have to do is call and I'll make time."

Roman felt like an intruder. "I'll fix you something to eat." Without waiting for a response, he practically ran for cover. He knew this wasn't his business. Instead, Roman focused on taking care of Brett. A slight hum of lust still lingered. Roman grabbed Brett's laptop and set it on the kitchen island while he cooked, multi-tasking. He needed to check on Brett's medical equipment so he could get around by himself. The hospital claimed it would arrive today, but they hadn't received a confirmation. Roman didn't mind driving to the medical supply store and picking everything up, but someone needed to let him know what to do. Brett wasn't the type to linger in bed for long. If this delay continued, he might be forced to find a reason for Brett to stay in bed. Otherwise, Brett would likely hurt himself trying to get back to work. He had more energy than any man Roman had ever met. Roman smiled at that thought. He could find an outlet for all that pent-up vitality. Roman still couldn't believe how Brett had been touching him before they had been interrupted. Damn, Brett made him hot.

"Hey."

Roman looked up from the laptop. Dean waited for his attention. Roman smiled. "Hey."

Dean returned his smile. He didn't look as cocky with the anger missing from his features. "Brett tells me you were with him in the accident. How are you holding up?"

No one other than Brett had asked about him. Roman appreciated the gesture. "I'm good. The airbag smacked me pretty good, but I have a thick skull, so no harm there. I'm just glad I was there for Brett."

Xavier appeared, wearing leggings and no shirt. Roman fought an eye roll. Xavier stirred Brett's soup. "What is this?"

"Homemade tomato soup. I'm just about to start on the grilled cheese."

Xavier tasted the soup. "It's good, but it needs

something. He started adding spices to the pot with no input from Roman.

Roman rubbed his temples and focused on Dean.

Inexplicably, Dean's expression had gone back to being hard. "I'm glad you seem to genuinely care. My brother has a lot of money. It brings out a lot of leeches." His gaze slid Xavier's way at that last bit.

Roman didn't know if he should be offended or if Xavier should. Either way, Roman couldn't fault the guy for looking out for his brother. He tried brushing off the remark. "That doesn't surprise me. Would you like to stay for lunch? Apparently, it's been made by a celebrity chef."

At his comment, Xavier's gaze slid his way. A hint of guilt crossed his features. "Apologies. I didn't mean to step on any toes."

Roman shook his head. He recognized he was being ridiculous by getting upset over Xavier helping. He wanted to be the one caring for Brett, but it would be stupid to not accept any assistance. "It's fine. I love your show. Have at it." He focused on Dean once more. "So, what do you say? Would you like to stick around? I'm sure Brett would love to have you here."

Dean's gaze swung between Roman and Xavier.

Xavier visibly tried looking humble. He failed on every level.

With a shake of his head, Dean tried for a smile. "A celebrity chef, huh?"

Xavier nodded. "I swear you'll enjoy yourself."

"I guess I've got some time."

Roman tried not to show his triumph. Getting to know Brett's brother was one more step into Brett's inner circle. It wouldn't be long until Brett wondered how he ever lived without Roman. His plan was coming together nicely. Roman couldn't fail.

# FIVE

FOR THE FIRST TIME SINCE THE WRECK, BRETT didn't feel too bad. His left leg was still pretty much useless and sore, but his head felt clear after a full night's sleep in his bed. Visiting with his little brother yesterday had been a huge help too. Sometimes, Brett forgot how much he needed what little family he had. Spending the day in bed with Xavier, Dean, and Roman while eating and talking nonstop lifted his spirits and made things seem not as bad today. Another highlight was the knee scooter that waited for him by the bed with a note from Xavier saying it had been delivered early this morning. Brett was ridiculously excited to try it out. It was so easy and made his life seem like a breeze compared to the way he had been struggling. The all-terrain scooter let him move from place to place with ease. He managed to bathe, dress, and do his hair with very few adjustments.

Once he had done as much as he could do to rescue his mangled appearance, Brett found himself still staring in the mirror. His face looked a mess. Both his eyes were black, and his left cheek still looked swollen. But oddly, he felt good. He had chosen a bright pink shirt and checkered shorts for the day. Brett loved being different. People either admired his courage or rolled their eyes at his eccentric style. Either way, he never left a neutral impression. He wanted people to see him and remember him. Right now, he needed to see Roman. It was time to get the man's vacation back on schedule. A hint of sadness wormed its way into his happiness at that thought. Roman would go home as soon as Brett no longer needed him. Hell, he might take one look at Brett moving around and leave today. Brett's shoulders squared. He would have to give Roman a reason to stay. At least for a couple more days. They had unfinished business. A wicked smile tugged at Brett's lips. If Dean hadn't shown up yesterday, Brett might have convinced Roman to finish some business yesterday. Damn. He needed to see Roman's sexy face.

With his knee balanced on the scooter and a smile in place, Brett rolled his way down the hall and into the bedroom he had assigned Roman. He didn't stop to think about his welcome. Childlike glee kept him moving. "Look what I can do." A completely nude Roman greeted him as he rounded the corner. Brett quickly turned his face away. He wished he had been quick enough to miss the sight altogether. Goddamn. So much delicious skin. "Sorry. The door was open, but I should've announced myself sooner or something."

A sexy chuckle floated through the air and washed over Brett. Roman crossed the room. Before Brett knew what would happen, Roman clutched his chin, turned Brett's face back his way, and captured Brett's mouth. It was carnal and heaven. Brett lost the ability to think and breathe.

Roman pulled away and swiped the moisture from Brett's bottom lip. "I find it odd that you never turn away from Xavier's nudity, but—with me—you act as if you've never seen a naked man."

"Xavier wants me to look at him."

A slow and sexy grin spread across Roman's lips. "So do I." He gently kissed Brett's nose—like trying to heal it before moving to Brett's bruised cheek. He whispered more confessions while his lips lightly brushed Brett's skin, seducing him. "I like to be watched." Brett felt Roman's lips shape a smile against his skin. "I think you do too." He ran his hand down Brett's stomach, stopping before he reached the waistband of Brett's shorts. "That's why you're wearing this hot pink shirt. You like it when people's eyes caress your skin. It makes me wonder what else you'd be willing to do while on display." Brett lost his breath. He was so turned on that he couldn't find the oxygen in the air. Roman turned away before Brett could panic and push him away. "Since you're up and moving, we should go out for breakfast. Do they serve anything other than coffee at that Back Porch place of Wrecker's? You should let your friends see that you're okay."

Brett's eyes ate up the sight of Roman crossing the room to dress. His every muscle bunched and rolled—like a predator ready to pounce at any moment. Roman was a dangerous work of art, but Brett realized something monumental. His killer body and beautiful face weren't why Brett couldn't stay away. Roman saw him. No one else saw him and it was fucking terrifying.

When he didn't respond, Roman turned his way, as he pulled on his clothes, giving Brett full view of his erection. Brett wanted it. He wanted all of

Roman. He hadn't called Roman because he knew the man would do anything for a price. Brett had called Roman because—deep down—he had known Roman would do him in ways no one else understood.

"They have pastries and breakfast breads," Brett heard himself answer—like he responded from a distance. He was totally screwed. Roman knew him. It was entirely possible this man would be his ruin.

———

ROMAN FREELY ADMITTED HE MOVED A LOT slower than necessary while pulling on his clothes. He made a show of flexing as he tugged his clothes in place. Brett openly watched. He made Roman proud. Roman had always suspected Brett would be like fire in his bed. Lots of people claimed to be kinky, but few truly knew the meaning. Brett would play. Goddamn. Roman had never wanted anyone as badly.

It hurt tucking his erection away and pretending his lust didn't matter. Right now wasn't the time, though. Roman still hadn't proven his worthiness. Occasionally, Brett still looked at him like he stripped for a living. He did, but Roman needed

Brett to see him as more than a toy before they slept together. Otherwise, he would never be more than someone to use and throw away in Brett's eyes.

"Let's see you in action," Roman said as he crossed the room fully dressed. "Set that baby in motion and show me what you can do."

A bright smile lit Brett's face, doing nothing to squelch the flush of desire still tinting his cheeks. "Probably not as much as I'd like but definitely more than yesterday. You'll probably still have to help me down the garage steps and into the car, but otherwise, I'm good to hit The Back Porch, if you are."

"Let's go." Wrecker would be on his honeymoon by now, so Roman was all in. Now that he knew Brett had been with Wrecker, he didn't feel quite as keen to ever see the guy again. Brett happily set his scooter in motion. He looked adorable—like a happy kid, rolling his way down the hall. When they reached the garage stairs, Roman easily plucked Brett from his feet and set him at the bottom of the three steps and handed down his scooter before closing the door behind them. He headed for the Range Rover again, since he knew it would be the easiest for him to help Brett maneuver in and out.

As he lifted Brett into the passenger seat of the

SUV, Brett shocked the hell out of him by kissing him. He leaned forward and pressed his lips to Roman's, as if testing the waters. When Roman leaned into the kiss, Brett opened his mouth over Roman's bottom lip. Roman tried to protect Brett's foot, but he lost himself. He dragged Brett closer while pushing his thighs apart to make room for him to get as close as possible. Brett pulled his hair and bit his bottom lip. Things turned into an inferno so fast that Roman threw out every plan he had to slowly seduce Brett. Before Roman could start tearing off clothes, Brett's kiss slowed and softened. He went from being a wildcat to tender in an instant. Roman wasn't any less seduced. In fact, he wanted even more than before. Brett's body wasn't enough. Roman craved his soul. He knew himself well enough to know he wouldn't stop until he had it.

"You're still sexy, but I miss the long hair." Brett sounded every bit as turned on as Roman felt.

"I'll grow it back out for you."

Brett chuckled. The sound was soft and sexy against his lips as Brett swiped another sweet kiss across Roman's mouth. Too late, Roman realized he sounded like he intended to stay. He wasn't sure yet if that was the case. First, he needed to win Brett's heart. That might not be as easy as he would like.

Brett could have anyone. He had no reason to settle on Roman. Roman would have to give him a few. That might be harder than he liked, since he didn't have much time left. He couldn't stay in L.A. forever. Roman had a job to get back to, but he would give this his all in the little time they had left. He couldn't give up now.

---

BRETT SPENT THE RIDE TO THE BACK PORCH trying to fight the overwhelming desire to climb Roman like a tree and fuck him. Hurt foot and all. He couldn't recall a time he had been this horny without relief. By the time they reached the coffeehouse, he thought he might survive. Until Roman helped him from the car again, that is. Roman smelled too good. His skin felt too warm. He was too close. Brett couldn't deny the sexual attraction.

"Stop looking at me like that. You're too much of a temptation."

At Roman's admonishment, a smile snapped to Brett's lips. He didn't doubt he had been eating Roman alive with his stare. Brett felt pretty damn intense. Still, he had his pride. "I don't know what you're talking about."

The sexy rumble of laughter that fell from Roman's lips at Brett's lie had Brett near to panting. The guy was an incubus. Brett was sure of it. A sigh of relief washed over Brett as they cleared the coffeehouse doorway. The scent of fresh brew lingered in the air. Despite being owned by Wrecker and the memories the place wrought of loving someone who couldn't love him, The Back Porch still felt like a second home. He genuinely liked the people who frequented the place. Several people called his name and jumped to their feet to hug him, expressing relief that he would be okay. His throat swelled as he realized how many wonderful people he had surrounded himself with the past few years.

Dawson, Wrecker's new manager, found Brett and Roman a table that would be easy for him to maneuver. The moment they were settled and finished ordering, the vultures set in. As always, Remington and Roscoe were the first to approach. They were dark-haired, light-eyed, and equally beautiful. The pair had met their first day of high school and had been inseparable since. They were a couple, but they liked to play. As far as Brett could tell, they had attempted to sleep with everyone new at The Back Porch since the day the place opened. The pair succeeded more often than they failed.

"May we join you?"

Brett fought an eye roll as the pair spoke in unison. His irritation quickly faded at Roman's expression. He stared in horror as they kept him locked in their combined stares.

"Is this some type of cult initiation?"

Brett covered his mouth, trying to hide his smile.

Remington wasn't the least bit put off by Roman's tone. "Would you like it to be? I'm certain we can find a few... tasks you could handle."

"He's with me," Brett said, cutting in and hoping to save Roman.

Roscoe smirked. "Even better."

A charming smile snapped to Roman's lips. In a blink of an eye, Roman transformed, turning fake. He nodded Brett's way. "This one has my hands full, but thanks for the offer. I'm sure I'll regret passing up your proposition. You both seem exquisite, but Brett is already more than I can handle."

Brett had to look away. Roman was too much.

"Maybe some other time," Remington said as the pair left them alone.

Roman chuckled. The sound had Brett pressing a hand to his stomach as his gaze slid back Roman's way. Roman shook his head. "Well, that was something."

Brett felt a strange need to come to the couple's defense. "They're harmless."

"Everyone is harmless if your heart isn't in it."

For some reason Brett couldn't explain, he found himself leaning forward and falling into Roman's eyes. Roman had so many facets that Brett had yet to uncover. He needed more. "Are you saying your heart is never in it?"

Roman's mouth quirked in one corner. "We're not talking about me. Those two are harmless until they meet someone who thinks sex matters. Then their games become very real."

Brett hid his disappointment. He had hoped to learn more about Roman. "True. I guess they're pretty safe around this place. No one here believes in fairytale romances."

"I do, but modern-day fairytales don't exist. Life isn't that magical."

For a moment, Brett found himself speechless. When he added together everything he knew about Roman—the flirting, his job, and the general show he always put on for everyone around him—Brett didn't come away with a picture of someone looking for love. "You're a dangerous man."

A line appeared between Roman's brows. "How do you figure?"

Brett shrugged. "You could easily make someone see a future with you, but I don't think you really want that. If you did, someone would have swept you away by now."

To his surprise, Roman smiled. "Maybe someone already has."

That sucked the wind from Brett's sails. He sat back, putting some distance between them. Brett hadn't realized how close they had moved to each other, leaning over the table as if drawn by an invisible lure. Brett needed space now. It had never occurred to him that there might be someone back in Aspen who owned Roman already. This thing had started as a weekend business transaction. Neither of them had expected that wreck. There was a very real possibility that Brett had been kissing and feeling up someone else's man. He felt sick. Why was he always dumb? He knew why he was always people's last resort. Brett wasn't like Roman. He didn't have that spark that drew people closer.

Brett knew he needed to say something before he ended up looking like more of an idiot than he already had. "I look forward to hearing about this mystery man sometime."

Roman's face hardened. "Did you really just sit back, accepting that you might be some California fling?"

Discomfort had Brett's gaze sliding away. "It's not unreasonable to think you have someone amazing back in Aspen. It's also not farfetched to think of myself as disposable. I'm always the guy on call. I need to check my accounts. My company is probably already falling apart at the seams. I can't imagine my clients will be too thrilled with their impressions this month." Brett dug out his phone and tried burying his horror by working. He couldn't believe he had let Roman get so close.

Roman's hand covered Brett's phone, bringing Brett's gaze to his. He looked sad. "I'm the stripper." Brett held his breath. Roman looked too serious. Brett needed to hear more. Roman didn't let him down. "I'm supposed to smile and drop to my knees for the right price. It doesn't matter that I don't actually do that last part. That's what everyone who meets me thinks of me. I don't meet people who are looking to build a life. I'm..." Roman seemed to fight for a fitting term before obviously settling. "Candy, I suppose." A sad smile touched Roman's lips. "I guess that's why meeting you struck me so hard. From the first moment, you've never treated me like a plaything. Hell, you don't even like me."

"I like you."

Something sweet flashed in Roman's eyes at Brett's confession. "Then put your phone away and spend some time with me. I can't stay in California forever. You'll still be amazingly successful long after I'm gone."

A wave of sadness washed over Brett at the thought of Roman leaving to never be seen again. He needed to use his time wisely. That way, Roman wouldn't forget him. Brett set his phone aside. "Tell me about yourself. I want to hear about your life."

A bright smile lit Roman's face. He slid his hand across the table palm up. Before Brett could take it, Jeremy, another regular, appeared beside their table. He only had eyes for Roman. "Hi."

Roman's smile slipped a hair. "Hello."

Jeremy rubbed the back of his neck, looking nervous. "Would you like to have lunch sometime?"

To Brett's surprise, Roman scowled. "What's the deal with this place? Is Brett invisible?"

Jeremy's gaze slid Brett's way. He looked even more nervous than before. "No." Horror touched Jeremy's features as he held Brett's stare as the truth obviously dawned. "Oh my gosh. I'm sorry, Brett.

You never date anyone. I just assumed he was a new client."

Brett waved off the apology. He knew Jeremy to be a tender-hearted guy. Jeremy wouldn't purposely approach anyone else's date. "Don't worry over it, sweetie. You're right. I don't date." He stole a quick peek Roman's way before adding, "Plus, Roman is ungodly gorgeous. It was fair to assume he could be famous."

Jeremy's shoulders fell—like a weight slid from them. "That's very true. You're a lucky guy. I'll leave you to your breakfast."

Brett smiled and nodded. He waited until they were alone again before looking Roman's way. Roman stared at him with an intensity that took Brett's breath. "You're a hit," Brett said, hoping to hide his sudden onset of nerves. He swiped his suddenly sweaty palms on his shorts. "Jeremy is very shy. You should be flattered he stepped out of his comfort zone to meet you. I expected half a dozen others here would have approached you first."

In a flash, before Brett could register what happened, Roman came to his feet. He didn't stop there. Roman climbed onto his chair. "Excuse me, everyone." The coffeehouse fell silent at Roman's loud words. Brett couldn't wrap his mind around

Roman's actions. Roman wore the same smile he always wore when putting on a show. It struck Brett that he knew that now. He could tell the difference between the real version of Roman and the showman. His mouth went dry as the truth sank in. He was the only one who got to see the real Roman. That didn't explain why he stood on a chair now. Roman didn't drag things out. He touched his chest. "I'm Roman. I'm with this guy right here," Roman said, pointing at Brett. He said the words so loudly and comically that no one could possibly be offended. "I just wanted everyone to know that so you can know how goddamn lucky I am that he not only wastes his time and affection on me, but also that he's still alive and well. That's all." Roman leapt from the chair, grabbed Brett's hand, and loudly kissed it while everyone still watched. Several people made sounds like they were moved by Roman's gesture while a few laughed at his audacity. Brett couldn't stop staring at him in shock.

Roman settled back down in his seat, but he held tight to Brett's hand. "Okay. Where were we? Oh yeah. You asked about my life. Well, let's see. I was born in Kit Carson, Colorado, which is East of Aspen. My parents still live there." Brett stared in awe as Roman spoke, as if nothing happened. He had spent so much time being Wrecker's booty call that he didn't know how to feel now. Roman had publicly claimed him in a spectacular display. Brett felt... stolen—like Roman had swept him off his feet when he hadn't been looking. He had to force himself to listen to every word Roman said because he was completely floored.

Roman kept talking, oblivious to Brett's plight. "My dad loves golf, so they travel a lot so he can try out different courses. Mom is a gay rights activist. She owns more pride gear than the factory that makes the stuff. I've been going to parades and rallies since I was born."

Brett found himself snagged. The shock faded. They were together. He wanted to know more. "Obviously something drives her."

Roman nodded. "My grandmother's brother was an out and proud gay man when it wasn't anywhere near as easy to be so. He never had any kids of his own, so he doted on my mom. They were very close. He died from complications due to AIDS. She said he wasn't treated with the dignity he deserved, and it lit a fire inside her. His life mattered. She won't stop until everyone knows it."

"That's very sweet. I'm guessing you didn't have to suffer the coming out most people do."

A bright smile lit Roman's face. He snorted. "You'd be right. Growing up, I would be like, she's hot. Damn, he's sexy. They look nice today. Mom would just smile and be like, well, pick one then. You're not limited. She's pretty amazing. She'd love you."

Brett smiled at the thought. A shot of longing hit. "I do miss being hugged by my mom." Brett froze. He couldn't believe he had confessed such a thing.

Roman's smile fell. "Has your mom passed?"

"No." Brett tried for a smile and failed. "She doesn't really speak to me anymore." He tried starting from the beginning so Roman would understand. "We were a military family and moved all over the world. I was the new kid at school every single school year and sometimes more often than that. In our house, kids were seen but not heard. We were expected to blend into the background and not rock the boat. By the time I was seventeen, that was getting to be way too hard for me." Brett motioned toward his bright clothing. "I'm not the fading-into-the-woodwork type. At first, I secretly took my eccentricity online. I started a YouTube channel where I played video games and talked about life. Before I knew it, I'd made a ton of money. We were living in Georgia and had been for two years. That was the longest we had stayed anywhere. Dean was fifteen and he had finally found his place after years of us being dragged around. We were happy. Then they dropped the bomb. Dad had been re-stationed. We were moving to Germany." Brett shook his head, losing himself in the memory of that horrible time. "We had two months to pack and ship everything to a new country. I was pissed. Dean was devastated. Even though I was still six months away from graduation, I was only one month away from turning eighteen. So I put my foot down. I not only refused to go, I demanded they leave Dean with me. They were angry and refused. We spent the next two months fighting and tearing each other apart. In the end, they agreed that Dean's happiness meant more than staying together." Brett shrugged. "He's been with me ever since and my mom refuses to speak to me now." Brett skirted that last topic to save his heart. "I worried that moving to L.A. would be another jarring move for Dean after he graduated, but he was actually excited to move again by then. I hope I've given him a pretty good life." Discomfort had Brett quickly shifting topics. "What's your stage name?"

Roman's smile said he knew Brett's game, but he didn't call him on changing the subject. "Adonis."

A smile exploded across Brett's face. For some reason he couldn't explain, happiness overwhelmed him. "I've never heard a more fitting name for anyone in my life. Did you choose it?"

"No. The day I interviewed for the job, my boss, Ken, said he'd been looking for an Adonis. So that's me now. I've been working there for so long that I answer to both names."

"Adonis," Brett said again, testing the name on his tongue. He liked it.

Roman chuckled like a funny thought hit. "If you joined me there, you could be Midas. Everything you touch turns to gold."

Without thought, Brett rolled his eyes. "No one would pay to watch me strip."

"I would." Roman looked too serious. His heated expression made Brett's heart skip a beat. Before Brett could feel uncomfortable, Roman switched topics. "Tell me all about everything you're currently working on. I don't want to miss a detail of you."

Brett shook his head, trying to clear the cobwebs in his brain. Roman always managed to weave such a spell over him. His lips moved, spilling every minutia of his life while his mind churned with confusion. He hadn't expected this. The coffeehouse cleared as people headed off to their jobs. Only a few people lingered as time slipped away from him. Roman wasn't who Brett thought him to be. Brett didn't want him to leave. On some sub-level, Brett recognized he should be running for the hills. He wasn't, because Roman sat still and listened to him talk. In fact, he looked like he couldn't get enough of hearing about Brett's life. Brett wanted to know every detail of Roman's life too. Something expanded in Brett's chest. Some unfamiliar emotion bloomed as Roman toyed with his hand and stared into Brett's eyes. Brett wasn't scared, even though he knew he should be terrified. He didn't know how to feel.

## SIX

GIVING CREDIT WHERE CREDIT WAS DUE, ROMAN had to admit that Brett had grit. He fought valiantly to stay out of bed for as long as possible. Unfortunately, sitting too long at breakfast without his foot elevated had been a mistake. The horrible swelling and pain had ended with Roman carrying him to the car while some dude named Dawson followed them out carrying Brett's new scooter. Despite being worried about Brett's health, Roman couldn't complain about hanging out with Brett in bed all day. It had been nice. They behaved like teenagers, ordering takeout and getting crumbs in the bed while playing video games and talking all day. Roman wished he could stay longer. He didn't darken the mood by saying as much.

"I never pegged you as the type to scream obscenities at the TV while gaming."

Brett's eyes swam with laughter. "That one statement proves you've never watched my YouTube channel. Back when my channel was nothing but me gaming with my friends, that's all I did was yell."

Roman shrugged. "Considering I'm at least ten years older than you, I think it's a generational thing. I never really got into watching YouTube videos. I'd rather play than watch other people."

"Ten years is not a generation." The heavy laughter in Brett's voice had Roman smiling so hard, his cheeks hurt. "Plus, there's no way you're ten years older than me."

"I'm thirty-nine."

Brett's eyebrows shot up. He visibly tried hiding his reaction. "Okay. So maybe you are. I'm twenty-seven." Brett looked thoughtful for a minute. "Are you serious, though? You don't look anywhere near thirty-nine."

Roman shook his head, trying to hide his laughter. "It's awful cheeky of you to assume that people look old at thirty-nine, but yes. I'm positive of my age."

Brett slid his hand up Roman's arm, taking his time as he outlined Roman's muscles. "I didn't say anything about thirty-nine being old. You have that fresh out of playing college sports body. That probably doesn't make sense to you."

"Yeah. I can't say I've spent too much time fucking athletes." Even Roman heard the bitterness in his voice. He couldn't think of any way to take it back, so he didn't try. Plus, Brett didn't look offended.

"You sounded so possessive just now." The heat in Brett's stare had Roman's mouth going dry. "What possible reason could you have for being jealous?"

Roman wanted to beat his chest and stake a claim, but he had no right. Instead, he slowly dragged Brett from where he sat leaned back against the headboard until he had the man flat on his back. Then he straddled Brett's body. Brett stared up at him—like he silently begged to be touched. "I envy anyone who's touched you."

"I'm right here." The softly spoken words held a challenge Roman couldn't miss, but Brett didn't know him. Not really. In most cases, Roman didn't give a shit about that. This one time, he cared. He didn't want to become an embarrassment to Brett. Brett was strong. Roman needed to make him proud. Brett wouldn't be proud if he knew the real Roman.

"Is it okay if I kiss you?"

A bright smile lit Brett's face. "You still have one kiss left that you can claim at any time, so yes."

Roman shook his head. "I want to save that one for later."

Brett expression turned serious—like he recognized Roman wanted to be a permanent fixture in his life. "I would very much like for you to kiss me."

With Brett's permission in place, Roman lowered his head. He lightly kissed Brett's cheek before moving to his mouth. This kiss wasn't like the ones they had shared before now. Roman found himself settling in for the duration. This wasn't about going further. This kiss was about staying put. They softly brushed lips and stroked tongues. Roman savored Brett. He knew he couldn't stay. Roman understood this wasn't his life. They were temporary. For a moment, though, he got to pretend. For the past week, he had been allowed to enjoy a life totally opposite to his. He had been important to someone amazing. Kissing Brett, stroking him, was a lot like being in heaven. It had been a long damn time since anyone enjoyed his company without seeking sex. The way Brett kissed him left no doubt that this would be their night, savoring each other without removing any clothes. It was the perfect end to his

L.A. trip. In fact, this was the best outcome he could have hoped to achieve. They would part as friends. As a pleasant memory. Roman would never have to see Brett's expression turn to distaste when he learned all of Roman's truths. To him, they would always be the chance at a real life that he had let slip away, but he cared. He felt too much for Brett to be more than this. He just hoped Brett didn't hate him in the morning.

BRETT STRETCHED. A MOUND OF COVERS weighed him down while a stack of pillows kept his foot elevated. The ache and stiffness reminded him he had slept through the night and forgotten to take his pain meds. Oddly, he didn't feel too bad. A smile tugged at his lips. Brett had a feeling that was mostly due to Roman. They had spent the whole night kissing, making out, and snuggling like a pair of teenagers until he had fallen asleep. Brett covered his face with both hands, hiding a ridiculous smile.

He hadn't known how much he needed what Roman had given. There had been no pressure to have sex. In fact, he had somehow understood that sex wasn't even on the table. They had simply been enjoying each other. No one gave him that. They had played video games and eaten junk food, for fuck's sake. No one had expected him to take them to a nice restaurant or meet them at their place after work. Roman fell somewhere in between the two types of dates he had grown accustomed to enduring: people using him for money or sex. Roman had wanted just him. His time. Brett's throat unexpectedly swelled. He wanted more.

Brett tossed back the covers. The TV still showed their paused game. Their food trash still sat on the side table. The room was empty. In fact, the whole place felt bereft of life. Brett dragged himself into a sitting position, wincing as his left side protested the move. As he reached for his phone to check the time, his gaze landed on a note leaned against the lamp. His name had been scribbled on the outside.

Brett knew before he read the letter what it would say. Roman had gone home. He should have known his kisses were a goodbye.

*Brett,*

*I didn't want to ruin our last day together by telling you I have to go home. My job won't hold my position for long if I keep missing days. Even though I have to leave, I can still help you out online with your* workload. You don't need to jump back into working with both feet. After all, you still only have one good one. I don't want to log in to your accounts without your permission, but if you'd like my help, please say so. Who am I kidding, right? You won't ask for help. Damn. I miss you already. For the record, I also didn't want to ruin our last night together by making love to you, even though I really wanted to. The last thing I want is for you to think all this has been some elaborate scheme to get in your pants. Plus, you really wouldn't want me if you knew me at all. I like you a lot, though. There's nothing I want more than to stay, but real life calls. I have to stop dreaming and get back to it. While I don't have a lot of bills, they still have to be paid. I really hope you still want to talk. My life has been pretty quiet since Mason married Falcon. Meeting you has been a definite highlight in my life. I don't want this to be goodbye, so I won't say that. Instead, let's say until next time.

Roman

P.S. You still owe me one kiss at any time of my choosing, so don't be trying to wiggle out of our deal.

Brett wanted to smile and cry. He had never been more torn in his life. It wasn't like he hadn't known Roman had a life in Aspen. Between Brett's wreck, hospital stay, and the few days he had been home, Brett had kept Roman over a week. That was asking a lot of someone who had a job they were expected to be at every day. Yet Roman hadn't complained. He had simply been as amazing as humanly possible every step of the way. Roman had given Brett way more than he deserved. It didn't seem fair to lament the man leaving now.

While feeling ridiculous, Brett swiped at his cheeks. The pain meds were making him weepy. He snagged his phone and checked the time, his messages, emails, and social media accounts. Nothing held his attention. He looked at things without actually seeing anything until a pattern emerged, distracting him from his misery. Brett lost himself, looking through his stats and past messages. His stats and payouts hadn't plunged since the accident—like he had been expecting. Instead, his interactions had soared. View counts were up and therefore payouts were higher. Brett scrolled back to the day after the accident to when Roman had introduced himself on all Brett's media accounts. He had given updates, responded to messages that Brett would have ignored, and chatted with people on every outlet. Roman had skated the line, keeping Brett's privacy while letting everyone know Brett would be fine and back better than ever in no time.

He had directed viewers to old videos they might have missed and promised more would be on the way. While Brett had been oblivious, Roman had been fucking amazing. Brett was more than blown away. He felt blindsided, but not in a bad way. Except he thought he might have just let the greatest person he had ever met slip away in the middle of the night. That was a horrible revelation.

Honestly, Brett had never been more confused by anyone. How had someone so seemingly feckless flown beneath his radar? The man had so much talent. If he could run Brett's accounts this competently, he could take over the world. Brett didn't understand why he hadn't. For the first time, Brett felt truly resentful of his fucked-up foot and ankle. He couldn't chase after Roman the way he wanted.

Instead, Brett settled back down to rest. He would never get better if he didn't try. Plus, he needed some time to think. Just because Roman hadn't turned out to be the guy Brett had always thought him to be, that didn't mean they could be together. Roman lived in Aspen. That wasn't even an option for Brett. Long-distance relationships didn't work. It was possible this last week was all they would ever have. That didn't mean he planned to give up without exploring this further. Roman wouldn't get away from him this easy. Brett just needed a few more weeks to heal, then Roman wouldn't know what hit him. A smile pulled at Brett's lips as a memory hit. Roman had claimed there were no modern-day fairytales. It just so happened Brett had enough money to prove that theory wrong. Even if they didn't end up together, Brett could give Roman a fairytale life. Maybe he would. After all, he was in the business of making dreams come true. He could conjure some magic for a man who had shown himself worth the effort. Brett hugged the covers tighter. He could make Roman smile.

# SEVEN

Sometimes, life left a bitter taste in Roman's mouth. While he hadn't expected to find himself magically in a relationship with Brett, he also hadn't expected to never see the man again. Roman had truly hoped his letter would take some sting from him sneaking away. He thought Brett would understand he didn't want their final day together to be clouded by the knowledge he would soon be gone. Maybe the radio silence had nothing to do with his sudden departure. After four weeks and no word, Roman had to concede that maybe he had imagined their growing feelings. Maybe it had been one-sided. It wasn't like Roman would know. He had never felt so much for anyone.

Roman's phone rang, startling him back to

reality. "Shit." Nothing smelled worse than burned eggs and Roman had lost himself in thoughts of Brett... again... and let his dinner burn.

With a growl, Roman tossed his frying pan into the sink and dug out his phone. Xavier's name flashed on the screen. He answered while trying to clean up his mess.

"Hello?"

"Hey there, gorgeous. How are you today?"

Roman stared at the huge mess in the sink, feeling pretty fucking low. "Peachy. How are you?"

"Oooh. What's with the desolate tone? Did you not get my invitation?"

"I must've missed it."

Xavier tsked. "Check your inbox, my dear."

Roman switched the call to speaker phone and checked his email. There was one from Xavier in a long line of junk from more than a week ago. He clicked the email and quickly skimmed the contents. "You want me to guest star on your show?"

"Of course, sweetie. Can you imagine the two of us side by side in the buff? We'll break the internet."

Despite his depression, Roman smiled. Xavier didn't possess an ounce of modesty. "When is this episode and what are we cooking?" He eyed the blackened eggs and wondered if he should even be entertaining this idea.

"In two weeks and I'm thinking something pretentious."

Roman's smile grew. Xavier was an acquired taste. Roman had truly come to adore the man during his time at Brett's. He understood how the man had burrowed his way into Brett's heart and ended up living in Brett's home. That thought was a huge reminder. Xavier lived in L. A... with Brett. The idea of being near Brett again was enough to have Roman agreeing to anything. "Okay. I'm in."

"Yes. We are about to take over the airways."

"How's Brett?" Roman asked before Xavier got too carried away.

"He's good. They moved him to a walking boot yesterday, which really makes him insane. He's having a hard time adjusting. So he's a bit cranky, but he's making it. At least he can drive again. That's lifted his spirits a bit. Oddly, his brother, which I didn't know existed, is suddenly always here. He's been a big help."

Roman mused over Xavier's bitter tone. "Do you not like Dean?"

Xavier huffed. "He doesn't like me. That's just not normal. Everyone likes me."

A chuckle escaped Roman. "Not liking you and just not wanting to fuck you are two different things. You know that, right?"

"No. That sounds like some made-up bullshit to me."

Roman shook his head while fighting back laughter. He had never met anyone as conceited as Xavier, and considering his job, that was saying a lot. Thinking of work had him looking at the clock. A sigh stuck in his throat. "Sorry to cut this short, but I have to get ready for work. I'll get back with you in the next couple of days and hammer out the details for the show. Thanks for the invite. It sounds like fun." It really didn't, but this would get him closer to Brett. That was all Roman cared about.

"Of course. Have a great night at work and rest assured I'll harass you again later if I don't hear back."

Even though Roman laughed, he didn't doubt it was true. "Talk to you later."

"*Adjö*," Xavier said, disconnecting their call.

Roman slipped his phone into his back pocket as he stared into space. Two weeks. Thanks to Xavier, Roman only had fourteen days standing between Brett and him. He could survive that. Possibly. Damn. Roman didn't understand how Brett had crawled under his skin like this. He had known there was something special about Brett. Roman just hadn't expected this longing to be with Brett that kept swelling in his chest. He wanted to drop everything and move back to L.A. Roman fought the urge to stalk Brett like a complete psychopath. It wouldn't be hard. He knew all Brett's passwords online. Roman could really get crazy. That was not what he wanted, though. He needed Brett to feel the same. Roman's heart demanded that Brett feel equally as insane about him. If Brett wasn't willing to call or text him, he damn sure wouldn't drop everything to come to Aspen to properly stalk Roman. Not that Roman expected that. He just wanted Brett to be willing to do it. Roman wanted to be special to him. With a growl, Roman headed to his bedroom to change. He had to work and no amount of overthinking things had solved anything yet. Maybe he would suck it up and be the one who called. His pride winced at the idea. Roman knew he was a mess. That didn't change a thing. He would keep waiting for Brett. However long it took. He would be here waiting.

Fuck. Things weren't going Brett's way. When he had decided to go on this impromptu trip to Aspen, he hadn't considered his arrival time. Funnily enough, though, he had thought a lot about the possibility Roman wouldn't be alone when he got here. Instead, Roman wasn't home. Since it was late on a Friday night, Brett should have known that. Weekends would be the big money maker for stripping, he imagined. Yet that hadn't once crossed Brett's mind while making the drive. He checked into his hotel room while trying to decide his next move. Considering the late time, the sensible choice would be to wait until morning to go see Roman, but then he was back to chancing Roman not being alone. Damn. He hadn't thought this through. Brett had always been the world's worst about getting an idea and running with it. He wanted Roman, so he had set out to get him the moment his doctor cleared him to travel. There was one option on the table, but it was a risky one.

Brett needed info. He knew where to get it, but he hated to ask. The last thing he wanted was to look desperate. Unfortunately, he had no other choice.

Brett: *I need a favor from your husband. Please don't ask any questions.*

Falcon: *Of course. You know I'll always have your back. Whatever you need.*

Brett: *I need the address to where Roman works.*

There was no going back now. Brett held his breath and waited. Three little dots danced on his phone for much longer than necessary, making Brett wonder if Falcon kept typing messages and deleting them. Finally, a new message appeared.

Falcon: *If I can't ask questions, may I give you a warning instead?*

Brett: *I'd rather you didn't.*

Falcon: *Fair enough. It's 1132 Anglers Way.*

Brett: *Thank you.*

Falcon: *You might not want to thank me just yet.*

Brett: *Fair enough.*

This was something Brett had to do. While Brett went most places alone, he couldn't help but feel uneasy this one time. He never went to strip clubs. Brett didn't know if nude bars were the type of place people went alone. He also didn't know why the nearly silent nondescript warehouse-looking building made the hair stand on the back of his neck, but it did. When he passed strip joints in L.A., they had flashing neon lights and signs that left no doubts to what the place offered. This place didn't have any of that. In fact, it was so dark that Brett checked the address Falcon had given him twice before heading for the door. Part of him hoped Falcon had mistyped. Something didn't feel right. As he approached the door, he realized the windows were blacked out, making the place seem darker. That made sense. The huge guard standing outside also seemed logical. After all, someone had to keep out underage people.

The beefy dude with dark hair held out his hand, stopping Brett. "Member or visitor?"

They had members. The no signs thing made a little more sense. "Visitor."

The dude pulled a radio from his belt and spoke into it. "Visitor at the door." He eyed Brett. "It'll be just a second."

Brett nodded. His discomfort grew larger by the second. Finally, a blond guy in a suit opened the door. He too eyed Brett from head to toe before waving him inside. Brett followed on his heels. The low thump of music came from the distance.

"I'm Ken," the guy said, leading Brett inside a small and badly lit office. "Are you interested in a membership or are you testing the waters?"

Brett had no clue what that meant. "I don't live here. I only came to see Adonis."

Ken nodded. He didn't make eye contact. Brett supposed that was pretty typical. No one wanted to feel seen here. "It's two fifty for a private show. Plus, whatever you want to tip. You have to pay upfront. If you want to use a credit card, it'll show up as Ken's Repairs on your statement. So no worries about privacy."

The whole transaction felt shady as fuck, but Brett handed over his credit card. He could hardly come to Roman's work and not expect to pay to see him. Ken ran his card and then headed back out. Brett followed. The place seemed to be nothing more than a long series of hallways and closed doors. Ken led him inside one. It was dark.

"Wait here. Don't worry. We keep everything sanitized. Adonis will join you shortly."

Like that, Brett was alone in a dark room. He really couldn't see much of anything. There seemed to be some type of window with a dim light peeking around the edge. It only offered enough light for Brett to make out a chair. He really didn't want to sit on anything after the sanitized comment, but his foot throbbed inside his walking boot. Brett made a valiant effort not to touch anything too much as he sat. Before he could get too grossed out, the curtain opened.

Brett's jaw dropped. Roman sat on a throne on the other side. Nude. Hard. Dick in hand and stroking. There were sex toys of every variety surrounding him. He looked turned on and ready to go. When Roman spoke, his voice came through an invisible speaker.

"What's on the menu tonight?"

Brett didn't respond. He couldn't. None of this was expected. He had somewhat prepared himself to see Roman in a thong with oiled-up skin while people tossed cash his way, but this was something else entirely.

Roman smirked. "Don't be shy. I can't see you, but I can hear you." He stood, looking proud as he moved to a nearby male sex doll. It looked like a high-dollar cyborg. It was anatomically correct in every way. "Do you want me to fuck him, or is he fucking me tonight?" Roman stroked the doll's humongous fake cock at the question. He winked. "I can take it."

Despite his shock, Brett's body responded. He wanted to watch, but it didn't feel right. Goddamn, Roman was smoking hot, but still. They knew each other. It seemed wrong. "I didn't drive nine hundred miles for this."

Roman froze. His face turned toward what Brett suspected was a two-way mirror. "Brett?"

"Yeah." A nervous-sounding chuckle escaped

him. "Sorry. I said I wanted to see you at the door. I think there was a miscommunication."

Roman looked uncomfortable—like he really wanted to cover his nudity. Brett's chest hurt. He felt like he had violated their trust or something. "I don't think I should've come here. I wanted to surprise you, but not like this." Brett stood. He should leave. "I'm staying at the Black Run Lodge. Suite two ten, if you want to see me." Brett headed for the door.

"Wait."

Brett froze. He couldn't look directly at Roman. "Yeah?"

"Don't move, okay?"

Brett shifted nervously. "Okay." The curtain drew closed, plunging Brett into darkness once again. Brett wanted to run. His mind was a mess. He hadn't expected any of this. Roman was an exotic dancer, or so he had said. Brett had known that part and been fine with it. This wasn't the same thing at all. He felt... Brett didn't know how he felt. They weren't a couple. He had no right to balk. Yet, he felt cheated in some way he couldn't explain—like Roman would never and could never belong to him exclusively.

The door swung open and Roman stepped inside. The lights flared to life. He wore jeans and nothing else. The button was undone like he had rushed to get to Brett. That small detail saved Brett's sanity. Still, he had a hard time meeting Roman's stare.

"I'm sorry." Brett had no idea why he apologized. "I should have told you."

Brett's gaze finally moved to Roman's. He looked devastated. "Why did you lie?" Brett couldn't stop the question. It came out sounding every bit as hurt as he felt. "You told me you were a dancer."

"I didn't lie, exactly. If you had requested a lap dance, you would've gotten one. You must've accidentally used just the right words to get this service. This is a sex club," Roman explained, needlessly. Brett had figured that much out for himself. "Most nights, I dance in a cage in the main room until someone asks for my private services." Roman's gaze skirted away. "I told you that you wouldn't want me if you really knew me."

Brett's heart twisted at the surety in Roman's voice. He fully believed Brett would reject him now. "How much time did my two hundred and fifty dollars buy with you?" Brett didn't know why he couldn't hurt Roman and walk away. He just couldn't.

Roman's gaze returned to cautiously meet Brett's. "Twenty minutes."

"Will you come see me when you get off tonight? I brought a gift for you."

Roman nodded. "If you still want me to, then of course."

"I still want you there." Brett reached past Roman and turned off the lights. "Get back to your throne, Adonis. I want to see if you really can take it."

Roman's mouth slammed down on Brett's with enough force their teeth bumped. Brett's body burned as Roman's tongue roughly brushed his. It was over as quickly as it started and Roman was gone. Brett closed the door and returned to his seat. It was very likely he was a complete idiot, but he couldn't spurn Roman. Maybe when he made it back to L.A., Brett wouldn't speak to him again. He couldn't say he wouldn't overthink this. Tonight, though, he wanted to watch. He wanted Roman to meet him later. His body craved everything. Brett wasn't leaving Aspen until he got what came for —Roman.

Roman couldn't believe Brett was here. He hurried through the secret passageways where staff safely traversed the hallways to slip back inside his private playroom. Even though he felt a lot more self-conscious than usual, he quickly stripped and hit the control to the curtain. Roman wondered if Brett had really chosen to stay. He decided to act the way he always did—like no one else was there.

"You're incredibly beautiful. I've thought so since the first time we met."

The words filtered through the speaker, letting him know Brett still watched. He flashed the two-way mirror a seductive smile. "The feeling is most definitely mutual." The memory of the first time they met over a year ago sneaked in. Roman's discomfort slipped away as he moved to stand at the mirror. He pressed his palms against the cool surface. "I think about the day we met all the time." Roman might have been embarrassed by his confession, but the mirror gave the illusion of being alone.

"We barely spoke that day."

There was a hint of confusion in Brett's voice. Roman didn't know if he could explain. Still, he tried. "You were behind your camera, filming Falcon. All day long, you barely spared me a glance. That gave me the freedom to watch your every move.

Study your every expression." Roman stroked his cock. "I saw something in you that I don't think most people would notice. There's a reason you're so good at what you do. It's because you like to watch."

Roman moved to his throne and sat. He draped one leg over the arm and slid lower, exposing himself and leaving nothing to the imagination. "You see all the right angles without trying, because you love all things visual." Roman used one hand to squeeze his balls and toy with his asshole while he used the other to set a rhythm meant to please. He watched his reflection, but he saw Brett's face in his head. "Your stare holds more intensity than anyone I've ever met. I see you. I understand why your clothes are always bright and why you always know who will be a star just by looking at them. It's because you see people and you like to be seen every bit as much. Yet no one seems to notice you in the same way you see all of them, do they? So, you dress a little more outlandish all the time, just wondering if today will be the day they'll recognize you for who you are. Imagine if you joined me in here as Midas." Roman's lust skyrocketed at the thought. Pressure climbed his shaft. He pumped faster. "Imagine if you let people watch you while you straddle my hips. I see you for who you are. You should let other people see too."

Roman writhed. His body burned. He wanted to be inside Brett. Before Brett, people had bored the hell out of him. Brett made him feel like he had something to offer to someone. He could give him this. Set him free. "Tell me who you are, Brett. Are you Brett or are you Midas?"

"I'm yours."

The words were so calmly and surely spoken that they sent Roman over the edge. Pleasure shook him as jets of cum hit him in the chest. He gasped for air, but his eyes never left his reflection. Brett was there, on the other side of the mirror, watching.

"Suite two ten. Black Run Lodge. Come to me."

Roman's eyes fell closed as the demand caressed his ears. His breath stuttered from his lungs. "I'll be there."

There was nowhere he would rather be. He just prayed Brett was actually there when he got off work. He still had a few hours before he could leave. That was too much time for Brett to think. Panic started to set in.

"Are you still there?"

A sexy chuckle rumbled through the speakers. "I'm still here. I still have seven minutes left on the clock."

Roman jumped to his feet. He didn't care about

anything. He snagged his shirt and swiped the cum from his torso before tossing it aside. Roman didn't bother wasting time to dress. He raced to Brett's side of the room. This time, he didn't bother with the lights. Roman kicked the door closed behind him as he overcame Brett.

"I'm claiming my third kiss."

Brett came back at him every bit as hard as Roman went in. Their tongues clashed. Brett's hands were everywhere, caressing. Roman dragged Brett closer, needing to hold him. Four weeks apart had been twenty-nine days too long. Roman never missed anyone. He ached for Brett. He didn't understand it. Never had. They just fit. This was the one for him. He thought his heart had always known it. That was why they kept seeking each other out without reason. Just because Roman knew they were meant to be didn't mean Brett felt it. He could still run.

"Please be there when I come to you. Don't run from me."

Brett kissed him sweetly, making Roman's eyes burn. "I'll be there. I promise. Just hurry." He deepened their kiss again while holding Roman's face between his hands. "Jesus, please hurry," Brett whispered against Roman's lips.

A loud knock landed on the door. "Time's up."

Brett startled in his arms.

Roman soothed him, rubbing his back. "Don't worry. He won't burst in here. I'll see you in a couple of hours. Sooner, if I can swing it."

Brett traced Roman's jawline one final time before pulling away. "I'll be waiting."

With his heart in his throat, Roman watched Brett slip from the room. He knew this could still go wrong in a million different ways, but he never dreamed Brett would accept this side of him. He needed to get this night done so he could be with Brett. They still needed to talk. A smile pulled at Roman's lips. Brett had shown up, though. He had followed Roman to Aspen. His brow furrowed. Why in the hell had Brett driven? Roman shook his head at the random thought. It was possible they hadn't cleared him to fly yet. In a flash, Roman went back to smiling like an idiot. Brett looked adorable in his walking boot and baggy as hell purple pants. Where did he find such crazy clothes? Roman couldn't wait to strip them away. He already counted the minutes.

# EIGHT

Brett thought he should probably be pacing the floor and chewing his nails. None of that happened. Instead, his mind churned, turning over Roman's words. Roman claimed Brett wanted to be seen the same as he saw others. Maybe that had some truth to it, but the rest of what Roman said was what he couldn't shake. Roman wanted him to climb inside the mirror as Midas. Straddle his hips while people watched. A pant escaped Brett. His current level of arousal was off the charts. He didn't think he was brave enough to do what Roman did. Surely there wasn't a secret exhibitionist living inside him. Brett was a too skinny guy who didn't look anything like Roman. Roman had cut muscles and a godlike physique, and the fact that Brett's only concern was how he looked was mind-blowing. He should be horrified at the thought of people watching him like that. Except he wasn't. Brett's entire body ached with desire. While most of his lust was thanks to Roman's show, Brett couldn't deny some of his arousal stemmed from Roman's accusations.

A knock landed on his hotel room door. His heart skipped a beat. Brett took a steadying breath. He had a few surprises for Roman and he couldn't wait to see the man's face. Brett opened the door. He caught a flash of Roman's heated expression before Roman overtook him. Brett heard the door slam as his feet left the floor. Roman's tongue invaded his mouth as he tore at Brett's clothes. He didn't have many since he had been dressed for bed. Brett fruitlessly fought to catch his breath. Roman obviously hadn't come to talk.

Brett's back hit the mattress. He swore the room spun. Rough fingers probed at his asshole, coating him with lube, and fucking with Brett's mind. He had no clue how Roman managed to find lube in his frenzy. Brett switched between clawing at Roman's skin and scratching at the sheets. His body was on fire. Nothing mattered but the arousal. Before his brain had time to catch up, Roman was inside him. Then things slowed. Roman's touch turned to a caress. His body rocked against Brett's. He kissed Brett softly. Reverently. Brett's heart sighed.

Roman kissed a path to Brett's ear. "I've missed you." He thrust. "Goddamn, I've missed you."

Brett's throat swelled and his eyes burned. He could feel himself falling for Roman and it was terrifying. Brett had never been more frightened of the way someone made him feel. Roman changed angles and Brett saw stars. Everything ceased to matter beyond the needs of his body.

"Damn. Make that sound again."

Brett had no idea he had made any noises. There was no chance he could duplicate the sound. Roman thrust hard. Brett almost came from the ecstasy of his perfect stroke.

"Yes," Roman praised. "That's it. I want your cum coating my skin. Let me have it." Roman didn't stop hitting that perfect spot until the pressure won, tearing a cry from Brett. His body jerked as the pleasure rocked him to his core. A sexy-as-hell roar tore from Roman, making Brett's orgasm hit twice as hard. "Fuck," Roman growled against his ear. "You really are fucking perfect, aren't you?"

Happiness swelled in Brett's chest. Laughter burst from him with no permission from his brain. His entire body shook with elation. "That was the most well-prepared spontaneous sex I've ever had. Were you wearing a condom when you got here?"

Roman's breathless laughter brushed his ear along with a kiss. "I didn't want to waste any time and take a chance of you shutting me down. Like I said, I've never wanted anyone the way I want you."

Brett couldn't stop smiling as he ran his fingers through Roman's hair and caressed his back. He didn't let his mind wander and overthink anything. Brett simply savored the moment of their bodies molded with cum gluing them together. "I have loathed every second I haven't been able to hold you like this."

At Brett's confession, Roman's lips found his. Brett was in heaven, but a hint of reality intruded. He broke their kiss. "You didn't let me seduce you with flowers and wine."

Roman pressed his forehead to Brett's. "Baby, you seduced me with bitchy comments over a year ago. Every other second with you that hasn't been like this one has just been torment."

Euphoria had Brett smiling like an idiot. "I've never met anyone else who gets turned on by bitchiness."

He felt more than saw Roman shrug. "It takes a certain level of passion to have that much fire. What can I say? You press all the right buttons with me. I just want to be with you."

The swelling was back in Brett's throat. He had come here the second his doctor had given him the okay to drive again, determined to sweep Roman off his feet. Instead, Roman kept blowing him away. Brett wasn't sure any longer which of them was doing the chasing, but Brett knew his heart had been stolen. There was no denying that.

---

As reality slowly came back to him, Roman realized he was probably crushing Brett. He rolled to his side before sitting up and tossing the condom in the trash. He had attacked Brett like a crazy man, and his heart still wasn't appeased, but he finally took a second to look at his surroundings. There were a few candles flickering beside a bouquet of roses. An unopened bottle of wine sat nearby. Roman blinked at the sight.

"Is that for me?"

Brett sat up and kissed his shoulder. "Yes. I brought you something else too." Brett sounded nervous. He had Roman's attention. Brett pushed to his feet and hobbled around the room, finding a towel to wipe away the mess on his stomach before trying to dress. Roman didn't like that. He wanted Brett nude. Thankfully, Brett only covered his body in the bare minimum of clothing. A pair of workout shorts and nothing else. He grabbed something from the table and motioned for Roman to follow him. "You might want to cover up a little so we don't get thrown out of here."

With a sigh, Roman pulled the sheet from the bed and wrapped it around his body like a toga. Brett's bright smile made his ridiculous choice worthwhile.

Brett limped for the door. "These past few weeks, I've been thinking about something you said." He opened the door. "You said there was no such thing as a modern-day fairytale anymore. I can't let you think that's true." Brett shifted nervously as Roman came to stand at his side. He passed a thick piece of plastic Roman's way. It took Roman a second to figure out it was a keyfob. Roman pressed the button. The lights flashed on a new-looking Land Rover. Confusion had Roman's gaze turning Brett's way. Brett bit his bottom lip, looking like he questioned his entire life.

Brett motioned toward the SUV. "It's yours. I

brought the title with me, already signed over to you and everything."

Roman tried handing the keyfob back. "You can't give me a car."

Brett shook his head, refusing the keys. "It's yours," he repeated, sounding firm. "I bought it for you. The last thing I need is another car."

Roman stared at the keys. He didn't know what to do. This was unfamiliar territory. "I'm not for sale." The words burst from him before he could think things through. It was too late. "I know it must seem that way, especially now that you've seen me at work, but you can't buy me."

Brett's expression closed, making Roman's chest ache. In a flash, Brett snatched the keyfob from Roman's hand and headed back inside. Without a word and while limping more than he had been, Brett dragged out his suitcase and started tossing things inside. In the middle of grabbing his stuff, he blew out the candles and moved on.

"What are you doing?" Even Roman heard the tightness in his voice.

Brett didn't look his way. "I didn't intend to have to drive another nine hundred miles back home. I guess I'd better get started now, since that seems to be the case. It's a good thing I didn't take any pain meds in anticipation of seeing you. Otherwise, I'd be stuck here with someone who thinks the worst of me."

A hint of shock wore off, allowing a few truths to sink in. Brett had driven nine hundred miles to give Roman a car. He might have been wrong about Brett's intentions. "I don't think the worst of you."

Brett snorted, but he didn't say anything else. He headed for the bathroom and flipped on the lights. Brett worked on repacking his toiletries. "You know, I've been doing next to nothing for the past month, trying to get better so I can come here and sweep you off your feet. When you never called, I guess I should've taken the hint. Still, you played me. I really thought with all your sweet talk and trying to get to know me, that you really were looking for a relationship with me. Pretty stupid, huh? That's me in a nutshell, though. I hung around in the background for Wrecker for years. He's by no means the first. I must have some invisible sign that says I'm stupid or something. For fuck's sake. Why do I have so much stuff?"

Roman closed the distance between them and wrapped his arms around Brett, trying to hold him together. Brett looked half a second away from totally coming unglued. "You're not stupid. I am."

Roman tightened his grip as he felt everything slipping away. For five minutes, he had thought they would be happy, and he had immediately fucked up—like always. In his panic, he rushed to explain. "In my profession, a lot of people have offered me some ridiculously expensive gifts to be at their bidding... sexually. Back in California, when I said there were no modern-day fairytales anymore, I meant no one stares into each other's eyes on a first date and falls in love. You don't hear about people accidentally brushing hands and knowing they've met the one. No one gets a fairytale wedding with a happy ever after. Well, I don't get those things. I guess other people do, but those things will never happen for me because I'm an exhibitionist at a sex club five nights a week. No one looks at me and thinks they want to spend the rest of their life with me. That just doesn't happen to people like me. No one wants to buy me a car for no reason other than to have me as their candy."

Brett lifted his chin. Their gazes met in the mirror. Brett's eyes shone bright with unshed tears, shocking Roman to his core. Brett sniffed. "I do. When I look at you, all I can think is that I could see myself with you for the rest of my life. You're who

I'm looking for. I don't expect you to let me buy you. I want you to let me love you."

Roman's mind went blank. The shock of the car had nothing on this. At least, this time, he wasn't dumb. He didn't release his hold on Brett, so Brett couldn't get away when he didn't respond immediately. He thought about all the feelings that had been stirring in his chest since arriving at LAX and seeing Brett for the first time in months. The memory of sitting across from Brett half the day in that coffee shop fluttered through his mind. He had been swept away while staring into Brett's eyes. Roman had thought he could spend the rest of his life with this man. He had been fighting to win him for good, because they were real. All his thoughts about them being meant to be weren't just fanciful musings. He was in love with Brett. "That seems fair, since I already love you."

Brett didn't say a word. Instead, he continued holding Roman's stare in the mirror, as if waiting for the other shoe to drop—like he didn't trust that anyone could love him without strings.

Roman swept Brett from his feet and headed back to bed. "Where are your pain meds, sexy? You're not going anywhere."

Brett clung to Roman's chest still looking like he

expected to be rejected. "I don't know. I haven't been paying attention to what I've been packing."

Roman settled Brett on the bed, unwound his sheet from his body, and covered Brett with it before going in search of Brett's meds. He started in the bathroom with no luck before moving to Brett's suitcase. Roman found them in the front compartment. "Here we go. I see they've lowered your dosage quite a bit."

Brett didn't respond. He watched Roman's every move from the bed.

Roman snagged a bottle of water from the mini bar and headed back to bed. As he sat on the edge of the bed, Brett's silence snapped Roman's nerves. "Did I break your brain by telling you I love you?"

"No." Brett sat up and accepted the pill and water. He didn't speak again until he swallowed his meds. "I like watching you and I'm in a lot of pain. I twisted wrong when I stormed back inside," he admitted with a wince.

Roman fought the urge to dig beneath the covers and check Brett's foot like he had a medical degree. Instead, he set Brett's water bottle aside and crawled beneath the covers with him. "Come here. Let my snuggles fix you."

The sigh of relief Brett released as he settled into

Roman's arms said a lot. Brett obviously still struggled with a lot of physical pain he tried to hide. With his head on Roman's chest, Brett stroked Roman's stomach like he tried comforting himself. Roman's guilt doubled over his reaction to Brett's gift. Before the desire to apologize profusely took ahold of his tongue, Brett beat him to it.

"I'm sorry I overreacted. I should've realized lots of people have probably tried to buy you over the years. I'm not special."

Roman kissed the top of Brett's head. "You are to me and you didn't overreact. I deserved your anger. Honestly, I don't know why I reacted like that. You deserve better from me."

Brett shook his head. "You want me to be different than everyone else, and—for a moment—my gift made you feel like I'm not. I get it. I want you to be different from everyone else, and—for a moment—your reaction made me feel like you're not." He felt Brett shrug like he hadn't just hit the nail on the head. "No one has ever fallen in love with me and I've never been in love before you. It makes sense that it would make me overly sensitive until I feel like we're secure."

Roman started to laugh, because Brett was always so goddamn logical, but then Brett's words sank in. "Wait. Did you just admit to being in love with me?"

Brett tilted his chin up and met Roman's gaze. "Well, yeah. I told you in the bathroom that I wanted you to let me love you."

The shock had Roman acting even thicker than usual. "Yeah but wanting to love me isn't the same as actually loving me."

A line appeared between Brett's eyebrows before clearing away. "Fair enough. I love you, and I know that it's real, because I would never humiliate myself by saying something like that this fast unless I felt it."

A smile snapped to Roman's lips. He really did love this sexy genius. "I believe you. No one in their right mind would put up with me unless they love me. I love you too." He dragged Brett up his body until he could go nose to nose with Brett. "Don't you dare threaten to leave me like that again."

Laughter flashed in Brett's eyes. "What will you do if I do?"

He hadn't thought that far ahead. "I'll cry, and trust me, you don't want to see me cry. It's ugly." Brett's laughter kept Roman talking. "Like runny nose and blotchy skin ugly. I'll sit on the floor and hold your legs, refusing to let go, while I wipe snot on your expensive pants."

"Ewww, stop." Brett's body shook with laughter.

"You've never seen dramatics like mine. You'll have people calling child services on you. When the police arrive, I'll give them the big eyes and tell them how you've abused my feelings."

Brett shook his head. "You're ridiculous."

"Maybe I am," Roman said, tightening his hold on Brett, and turning serious. "Or maybe there's no low too low when it comes to keeping you. I've never missed anyone. I miss you all the time. This past month, I didn't call because I was terrified you didn't miss me, and that I would look like just another desperate guy in your life if I called first." He winced. "I was waiting for you to call."

To his surprise, Brett chuckled and kissed his chin. "Oh, we are a couple of idiots. I was waiting for you to call me first." Brett settled back down in Roman's arms as he made his confessions. "I feel like I'm always the weak one. This one time, I didn't want to be seen as disposable. I didn't want you to know I care."

Roman stared at the ceiling and shook his head. "Wow. We are a mess."

"It's not our fault, I don't think." Brett went back to stroking Roman's stomach. "I think we're just a little jaded." Brett sounded tired, which made sense.

He had driven from L.A. to see Roman and Roman hadn't gotten off work until two in the morning. Not to mention, Roman had given him some pain meds. No doubt, Brett probably held on by a thread at this point. A small smile passed over Roman's lips. He couldn't believe Brett had driven all this way to bring him a new car. That was the craziest slash greatest thing anyone had ever done for him. Brett was really amazing. He felt the tension drain from Brett. Brett's hand went still on Roman's stomach. Roman tilted his head to see Brett's face. Brett was out. Roman stared at him in awe. This amazing guy had fallen in love with him. Roman couldn't believe it. He wasn't sure he deserved Brett's love, but he would. Roman would make him proud. Somehow.

AFTER A SOLID NIGHT OF SLEEP, THE WORLD seemed a thousand times brighter when Brett woke in Roman's arms. They went to lunch. Roman drove, getting a feel for his new SUV. Lunch turned into Brett checking out of his hotel and moving his things to Roman's house. The day passed too quickly. Brett wanted to cling to Roman and beg him not to go to work, but he knew he had to be realistic. Just because they had exchanged I love yous, that didn't mean Roman would or could quit his job. Brett loved him. That meant loving all of him, even this part he hadn't found a way to be completely comfortable with yet.

"Come with me."

Brett tried to hide his distaste. "No, thank you. I'd be a distraction and that's a lot of hours to sit there, watching other men drool over you."

Roman's sexy smirk made him hard to resist. "You'd be surprised. There are a lot of distractions there. People don't usually sit and drool over me. A lot of people are there with their doms and subs, playing. Most of the members are just looking for a safe space for their kinks. It has little to nothing to do with me as a person. I think you should see that for yourself."

Brett pulled a face. On one hand, he knew Roman was right. If they were seriously going to do this thing, he needed to be okay with Roman's job. On the other hand, he didn't know if he was ready. "I don't know."

Roman straddled Brett's lap on the couch. He looked fucking delicious. Brett didn't want to let him go. "How about this? I'll leave you the Land Rover and take my old car. That way, if you decide to join me, you'll have wheels. At the door, let them know you're my visitor and I'll warn Ken to keep an out for you. That way, you don't get charged if you change your mind."

That seemed fair. "Okay. If you want, you can leave me your old car. It doesn't matter to me how I get there."

Roman shook his head and visibly tried hiding a smile. "I won't have you trying to get in and out of my small car with a boot on your foot. I've driven the same car for twenty years now. Another night won't kill me."

Brett rolled his eyes, fighting a happy sigh. No one had ever put him first like this. He didn't know how to react. Roman didn't let him overthink anything. He nuzzled Brett's neck before kissing his jaw. Roman's lips brushed Brett's cheek and moved to his mouth. Brett held his breath in anticipation until Roman's tongue stroked his. His kiss was slow and methodical, stealing all Brett's good sense.

"Ugh. I miss you already."

"Stay home. I'll support you."

Thankfully, Roman laughed at Brett's offer rather than getting insulted the way he had at being gifted the SUV. "Everyone wants you for what you can do for them. I just want you. Come see me. I'll be waiting." Before Brett could tell Roman no again,

Roman slipped from his lap. "I love you, gorgeous. If I don't see you up there, then I'll see you when I get home."

Brett swallowed the lump growing in his throat. "Okay. I love you too."

With a final heated glance his way, Roman left. For a long while, Brett stared at the door Roman disappeared through. Then he pushed to his feet and trailed through the house like an abandoned puppy. Roman's place was small but nice. It reminded Brett a lot of the many houses he had lived in as a kid. One large master bedroom and two smaller bedrooms. A kitchen that would be minuscule if not for having an area for a dining room table. As small as the place was, it felt empty as hell without Roman. He tried snacking and watching TV. Nothing held his attention. Three hours after Roman's departure, Brett found himself in the car and headed toward the club. He berated himself the whole way. This felt like a mistake. Even though Brett didn't consider himself the jealous type, he didn't know how he would feel while watching other people wanting his man. This might ruin them.

It was the same guard working the door again tonight. "Member or visitor?"

Obviously, they truly didn't see anyone as they

came in or left. The guy didn't seem to recognize him. "Visitor."

Once again, he pulled his radio from his belt. "There's a visitor at the door."

Ken appeared just as he had the night before. He eyed Brett from head to toe. "You're Midas, right?"

Brett smiled. He shouldn't find anything about this endearing, but there it was. "Yes."

"I told Adonis I would keep an eye out for you. I'll show you the way."

This time, Ken took an immediate right turn and the music got louder as the place became more like the nightclub he had been expecting. There were more people than the cars in the lot made it seem to be. Cages hung from the ceiling in the center of the room and leather couches outlined the edges, giving people a place to sit while enjoying the view. There was a bar in one corner. An odd mixture of clothed and unclothed people littered the room. Some people wore collars while others were on a chain. Blatant sexual acts took place in the middle of it all with no one seeming to notice or care. There was a guy getting blown and not a soul paid them any attention. Brett caught sight of Roman and then he couldn't see anything else. He knew the exact moment Roman spotted him. His face lit with an inner happiness that took Brett's breath.

Ken motioned toward an empty loveseat closest to Roman's cage. "Have a seat."

Brett nodded and sat. His gaze never wavered from Roman. While wearing only a thong, Roman's hips moved in time with the music inside his cage. He looked ten steps beyond sexy. Brett couldn't believe Roman was his. It seemed surreal that they were together. There was so much happening around them, but Brett couldn't see anything beyond Roman. If anyone there wanted Roman, Brett wouldn't know, nor did he care. Roman belonged to him. He could feel it in his chest. Brett's heartbeat thumped in his ears. His dick stirred with no permission from his brain. Roman tempted him like no one else ever had. He wanted the world to know Roman belonged to him.

"May I buy you a drink?"

It took Brett a minute to realize the offer was meant for him. He glanced over and into the lightest eyes he had ever seen. Brett opened his mouth to respond and Roman was there, brushing the man aside. "He's here with me."

The light-eyed man immediately turned away, seeming to almost bow out—like recognizing he didn't stand a chance against Roman. Brett didn't care about any of that right now. Roman looked sexy and he was barely dressed. Nothing but a few strings of material stood between Brett and paradise. Brett crooked his finger and pointed at his lap. Roman didn't hesitate to obey. He straddled Brett the way he had before leaving for work. A fine sheen of sweat made his body glisten. Brett wanted to feel him.

"I just realized something," Brett said as he ran his hands across Roman's waist, savoring the sensation of his slick skin. "Last night, I told you I wanted to see if you could take it the way you boasted, but you didn't try."

A wicked light entered Roman's eyes. "Don't threaten me with a good time. I'm unapologetically vers."

Brett smirked. "Me too."

"Goddamn," Roman growled, moving even closer. "I knew you were perfect." He claimed Brett's mouth and something inside Brett released. Some part of him that he kept hidden sprang loose. His fingers dove inside Roman's thong. He massaged, getting him hard until he could pump at Roman's cock, expecting results. It was like they were alone, but there was still a small part of Brett's brain that stayed aware they were surrounded by people. He just didn't give a fuck.

"I want to fuck you right here."

Roman's head shot up as Brett growled the words against his lips. He glanced around furiously, going as far as to lean to one side of the loveseat. A triumphant smile lit his face. "I thought they kept this place stocked, but I almost got worried." He flashed a condom and sample-sized lube at Brett. "Ask and you shall receive."

Brett licked his lips. Even with Roman's dick already in his hand, Brett questioned himself. He had gotten caught up in the moment, but now things seemed a little nuts. Until Roman kissed him again, that is. Brett forgot to be embarrassed. The front of his pants loosened. Roman openly stroked him with the same enthusiasm Brett had shown while setting Roman's cock free.

Roman's mouth moved to Brett's neck. He sucked and licked while rolling a condom down Brett's length. "Don't worry," he said as he coated the condom in lube. "I won't let anyone see you."

Brett thought that was an odd thing to say, but Roman shifted positions shoved his thong aside and impaled himself on Brett's cock. Brett's head fell back against the couch as pleasure rolled over him.

The way Roman braced his palms against the back of the loveseat combined with his large muscular body, he did somehow end up shielding Brett from most of the room. While Brett knew they were in the middle of a crowd, it didn't feel like it. Nothing mattered any longer but Roman's tight heat squeezing him. He kept stroking Roman's cock while Roman rode his dick. Brett stared into the face of the man he loved while everyone watched them claiming each other. It was empowering and sexy as hell. Roman belonged to him and now everyone knew it.

He urged Roman's face to his and bit Roman's bottom lip. Pressure climbed his shaft. He was turned on beyond painful. It was like he could feel the lust they caused around them, adding to his. "Tell me you're mine."

"I'm yours," Roman whimpered as Brett pumped faster, doing his best to get Roman off.

Something primal grew inside Brett. He could feel himself getting more possessive by the second. "When we're done here, you'll go find your clothes and come home. You're moving to L.A. with me."

Roman covered Brett's mouth with his, delving deep without responding to Brett's demands. Brett released Roman's cock and grabbed his jaw, forcing his face away. He held Roman's stare. "Do we understand each other? I'll find you a club in L.A. just like this one, if you want to play, but you're mine and I'm not going home without you. Am I understood?"

"Yes." There was so much desperation in Roman's eyes that Brett wanted to beat his chest, but first, he needed to please his man.

"Good. You feel so goddamn amazing on my dick. I need you to kiss me."

Roman fell on him, claiming Brett's mouth with a rough kiss as he used Brett's cock to pleasure himself. Brett couldn't breathe. He had never been happier and more turned on in his life. Pleasure beat at his crown. His fingers dug into Roman's ass. He pushed deeper and deeper, following Roman's cries. Roman moaned against his ear and his body spasmed on Brett's dick, sucking an orgasm from Brett. Brett cried out against Roman's shoulder, hiding his face as wave after wave shook him. He hadn't set out to fuck Roman publicly or get all possessive and demand Roman move in with him. His heart had taken control. Now that the intensity had passed, he worried he had gone too far.

Brett kissed Roman's cheek. "Are you okay, baby?"

Roman nodded against Brett's shoulder. "Just blown away."

Brett kissed his ear, hoping to soothe whatever he might have bent with his demands. "I'm sorry if I pressed too hard."

Roman lifted his head. Their gazes collided. "Are you taking it back?"

Brett shook his head. "I love you. You belong with me."

The way Roman rapidly blinked made Brett wonder if he fought tears. That seemed very unlike Roman, but he couldn't deny what he saw. "I'm not the kind of guy people keep and bring home to their parents."

A smile exploded across Brett's face. He had never been happier in his life. "My parents don't even want me, so fuck that. I want you forever. In my bed every night. As part of my life every day. I think you're perfect. I've never been prouder to be with anyone."

Roman traced Brett's bottom lip. His eyes followed the path of his finger. "The feeling is definitely mutual." Roman's gaze lifted and collided with Brett's. "Did you also mean what you said about finding a club in L.A.? Because I think this is more you than you've ever realized."

Brett couldn't stop stroking every place he could reach. He no longer cared or noticed they weren't alone. "I always mean everything I say, even if it's in the heat of the moment."

"I love you." Roman sounded like the words came from his soul and Brett swore he caught a glimpse of their future. They would be happy. Together, they had so much to explore. Brett couldn't wait to get started. Roman was his modern-day fairytale and Brett wanted his happily ever after. There was no time like now to spend the rest of his life with Roman. They would be beautiful. Brett would make sure of it.

# NINE

"Now that's a man."

Dean's gaze followed Peggy's line of sight to the two men wearing nothing but aprons.

"That's your son," Brett said, sounding like he found Roman's mom off-the-charts insane.

"Not him," Peggy said, lightly smacking Brett's arm and making no attempt to keep her voice down. She was a woman who gave zero fucks. "I'm talking about that big Swedish redwood next to him. Goddamn. That's a fine-assed man." Roman looked like he choked on suppressed laughter, but his mom wasn't finished. She cut her eyes at Brett. "Although I will concede you are allowed to think of my son as a man, since you'll be my son-in-law someday."

Roman blushed. "Mom. Jesus."

"I think she's great," Xavier said, calmly arranging pans and getting ready to start filming. It was the most subdued Dean had ever seen the guy.

Roman snorted. "You would think that, you big Swedish redwood."

Peggy seemed to be completely oblivious to anyone's discomfort or Roman's falsetto mocking. She turned Dean's way. "What about you, kiddo? Which one would you choose?"

Dean's gaze skirted everyone in the room. While his brother looked amused, Roman ignored Peggy like he had given up any hope of her behaving years ago. Xavier was the only one whose gaze was locked on Dean, intently waiting his decision. Dean took a breath. He didn't understand why Xavier was always so flippant with everyone except him. It was unnerving.

Dean tried ignoring him by focusing on Peggy. She looked so much like Roman with her blonde hair and hazel eyes. It was hard not to like her. "Roman feels too much like a brother, so that's just wrong. Xavier already has the rest of the world chasing him. He doesn't need another man wanting him, so I guess it's just you and me."

She smacked his arm. "Flirt. I like you."

Dean's gaze slid back Xavier's way. The man still

watched him. At least his apron hid the front lower half of his chiseled body. That helped a hell of a lot with ignoring him. There was no hiding his sexy gray eyes, though. Those were too beautiful for Dean's comfort.

"Now, what are you boys doing in June? Denver has a hell of a Pride event and I would love it if you came to stay with me to attend. We'd have a great time. My activist group has a float in the parade."

"Mom adopts everyone," Roman calmly explained.

"Like I said, she's great," Xavier said, still sounding more serious than usual. Only the fact that Xavier's light-colored eyes were locked on him made Dean realize he was staring again. Xavier's mouth lifted in one corner. "What do you say, Dean? That's a good six months from now. Want to go to Denver with me for Pride?"

Dean shrugged. "Anything can happen in six months, I guess."

Xavier finally looked away, but his smile turned wicked, making Dean wish he could read minds.

The camera crew came on set, saving Dean from any more questions. He had never been one to chitchat. He liked Roman's mom, though. She was nothing like his mom. Dean wished sometimes their parents hadn't stopped talking to them, especially since it was his fault. If he had just gone to Germany and been the good son, Brett wouldn't have felt like he needed to break ties with their parents to save him. The guilt was real and thick, knowing Brett no longer had a family because of him. Guilt aside, Brett had been an amazing parental substitute. Despite their loss, Dean wouldn't trade Brett for all the parents in the world. Peggy and Brett sat close and spoke in whispers, as if not wanting to interrupt the final setup before the show. Dean fought himself. He didn't want to look Xavier's way.

As his head started to turn that way, Xavier appeared at his side. He kneeled, speaking close to Dean's ear. "Will you stay after the show?"

Dean fought the urge to meet Xavier's stare. If he knew nothing else, Dean knew he couldn't show any enthusiasm over having Xavier's attention. Xavier had legions of men and women falling at his feet. Dean had no desire to add his name to that list. He tried to keep his voice free of emotion. "I don't know. Is there a reason you're asking?"

Xavier touched his jaw, urging Dean's gaze his way. The moment Dean focused on Xavier's gorgeous eyes, Xavier gave him the most heated look Dean had ever seen. "You know there is."

Dean swallowed. He had no idea how to stand against someone like Xavier, but he had to find a way. Xavier was the kind of man who chewed men up and spit them out. Someone like Dean could never hold his attention.

"Xavier, it's time to get started."

Dean fought a wave of relief as Xavier left him alone. That didn't stop his eyes from locking on to the man's sexy bare ass as he crossed the room.

"Completely hairless. Should've known," Peggy said against his ear. Dean covered his mouth, fighting a smile. She didn't quit. "He is a sexy one, though. Goddamn. Ten bucks says he likes it rough."

"He's conceited as fuck," Dean whispered back, incapable of stopping himself.

"*Mhmm*. With a body like that, I don't doubt it, but he still can't take his eyes off you. You only live once, kiddo. There's nothing wrong with a little fun."

"Maybe." That was the best Dean could do. He had a feeling Xavier's fun would lead to uncontrollable longing. Dean just couldn't see any scenario where one night with Xavier would be enough. Xavier was rich, famous, and sexy. Dean already knew he would want to keep him if he touched him. He was a greedy person. Needing his way had already lost Brett their parents. Dean had to stay disciplined. He wanted things too hard. Xavier was no exception. That was why he had to stay away.

---

BRETT COULDN'T STOP SMILING. ROMAN'S MOM had come into town for a visit two days earlier, coming to watch Roman's third guest spot on Xavier's show. She was a nut and he adored her, but she wasn't the only reason his happiness level was off the charts. Roman always looked like he belonged on Xavier's show. Brett wanted Roman to be happy in L.A. As promised, they had started looking for a club where they could explore Brett's newfound exhibitionist and voyeuristic tendencies. He had also handed over his social media handling to Roman, since he was a natural and needed something to keep him busy. The last couple of months had been amazing. Sometimes, Brett had sudden panic attacks when the fear of losing Roman would strike from nowhere. Even with everything he had worked for, Brett never had so much to lose since falling in love with Roman. Their life together was the most beautiful thing he had ever experienced. He genuinely hoped Xavier's third invite meant he might be considering bringing Roman on as a full-time cohost. Every little tie Roman made to this town was another reason for Roman to stay. Brett still didn't think he was enough incentive to stay. He stewed over his thoughts for so long, he missed a majority of the show.

"We saved a special treat for last," Xavier said, making Brett realize exactly how long he had been lost in his thoughts. "As you all know, we use a lot of TV magic on the show by cooking food in advance so we can show you every step in a timely manner. This final delicacy is different. While it was prepared in advance, it wasn't done so for TV illusions, but another enchanting piece of wonder." Xavier opened the refrigerator and took out a small cake box. He passed it Roman's way. "I believe this is your part."

Roman glanced down at the cake and chuckled. He showed the cake to the camera. Brett had to look at a nearby screen out of camera view to read the cake. He covered his mouth to hold in his happiness. "Will you be my cohost?" was written in cursive on top.

With a smile, Roman sat the cake aside. "I tell you what, Xavier, I'll give you my answer after I get mine." He turned around and opened the fridge, pulling out another cake.

"Oh, lord, my baby is showing his booty."

Everyone laughed at Peggy's interruption. Brett thought she had been pretty damn well-behaved up until this moment, considering her bubbly no-fucks-given personality.

The camera followed Roman as he headed Brett's way. He spoke to the camera, as if talking to his audience as he crossed the room. "People don't usually see behind the cameras, but I have some special people here with me today. My mom, Peggy, is here. So is my gorgeous boyfriend, Brett. Brett's brother, Dean is hanging out with us too. I asked all of them to be here today for a reason."

Brett's confusion skyrocketed. Xavier had been the one to issue invitations to everyone, or so he had thought. Then Roman handed Brett the cake. Brett stared down at the white confection, blinking at the sight. There was nothing written on the cake this time. Instead, a diamond and platinum ring sat upright—like the cake served as a ring box. Roman dropped to one knee. Peggy squealed, nearly rupturing his eardrum. Only the shock kept him from reacting.

"What do you say, beautiful? Will you make an honest man out of me?"

"Boy, that'll take some work," Peggy said,

bringing Brett back to life, pulling him from his shock.

He nodded, trying to find his voice. "Yes. Every day of the week. Yes."

Peggy squealed again. This time, he definitely lost some hearing. He heard the congratulations from Dean, Xavier, and the crew, but Brett couldn't see anyone except Roman. This amazing man really wanted to marry him. He had planned this and gotten down on one knee. Brett was more than humbled. He thought he might cry. His throat burned. He couldn't stop stroking Roman's face.

"I love you so much."

Roman gathered him in his arms. "Don't cry, baby. I love you too."

Brett was too moved to be embarrassed as he buried his face against the crook of Roman's neck.

"This was really sweet, baby doll, but you could've worn some pants."

Brett choked on a mixture of tears and laughter at Peggy's claim. "It was perfect. I love your naked booty," Brett whispered against Roman's skin.

With a laugh, Roman held him tighter. He had never dreamed this could be his life. If he had, he never would have pictured himself ending up with Roman. He couldn't have predicted this tremendous love that came from nowhere and consumed him. But Brett wouldn't give this up. Not now. Not ever. Somehow, he had stolen Roman's heart. Brett would never give it back. They were forever. No take backs.

Keep an eye out for the next Candied Crush, *Beautifully Moved.*

Please consider leaving a review at the retailer where you purchased this book. Reviews really help with a book's visibility, which allows me to continue writing more stories. Thank you, Charity.

## ABOUT THE AUTHOR

Charity Parkerson is an award winning and multi-published author with several companies. Born with no filter from her brain to her mouth, she decided to take this odd quirk and insert it in her characters.

*Eight-time Readers' Favorite Award Winner
　　*2015 Passionate Plume Award Finalist
　　*2013 Reviewers' Choice Award Winner
　　*2012 ARRA Finalist for Favorite Paranormal Romance
　　*Five-time winner of The Mistress of the Darkpath

Connect with her online:

—Sign up for my newsletter: http://bit.ly/CharityNews
　　—Join my readers' group on Facebook: http://bit.ly/CharitysTribe
　　—Website: charityparkerson.com

—Facebook:
facebook.com/authorCharityParkerson
facebook.com/TheMenofSin
—Twitter: twitter.com/CharityParkerso
—Instagram: Instagram.com/sinnerauthor

www.ingramcontent.com/pod-product-compliance
Lightning Source LLC
Chambersburg PA
CBHW060229180626
46813CB00007B/3007